MOUNTAIN SHADOWS

Noelene Jenkinson

Chapter 1

Piper Thorne yawned behind the wheel of her early model Holden Commodore and gripped it tighter. It had been over three hours since she left the Victorian south coast, her current temporary sanctuary, to head north into the Wimmera, but she was almost home.

While it was often months between visits back to her family and country, with each passing kilometre she found returning was healing, simply by being in her motherland where she belonged. She was proud of her indigenous heritage. It was a part of her and she always felt her ancestors watching.

But she needed to stop. Take a break. Coincidentally, the Coach Roadhouse sign came into view so she slowed, signalled and turned in. After refuelling her beloved old guzzler, she found a park and unwound her stiff body to stretch, gazing at the surrounding familiar bush landscape, breathing deeply, feeling her happiness overshadowed by the sad reason for this journey. Knowing she would never see her cherished grandma Thorne ever again but the forthcoming funeral and ceremonies would ensure the safe passage of her spirit into the afterlife.

Reluctantly, Piper set her nostalgic thoughts aside and wandered into the roadhouse to see waitress Holly Duncan's friendly face and beaming smile.

'Hey Piper.' Her expression shadowed and her brows dipped into a frown. 'Sorry to hear about your grandma. She'll be missed.'

Piper appreciated Holly's genuine sentiments. Despite an extensive search at the time, Holly's mother had gone missing five years ago with no news of her whereabouts ever since. It must be tough for the waitress no longer having a mother in her life and, as yet, no closure to grieve and move on. Although not close to her own mother, Piper's heart filled with compassion.

Piper's wider family and relations would all be gathered and an abundance of food would already have arrived at her parents' house on Jack's farm where her father Jimmy was manager. But she ordered a large takeaway serving of Gracie Townsend's casserole special of the day anyway and a strong black coffee for herself.

Piper didn't linger, keen to continue the remaining few kilometres of her drive home.

Half an hour later as Piper turned off the main road to the farm cottage, she noted it was already surrounded by a dozen vehicles. There would be crowds inside, noise, crying and food. Understood, because grandma Thorne had been an Elder, recognised because she had earned community respect through her lifetime of wisdom and teaching, passing down her knowledge and experience to ensure cultural continuity.

By nature an introvert, Piper braced herself for the meetings and renewals. Not by choice, of all her siblings and cousins, she was the outsider, occasionally drawn back but contented with her individual roaming life.

Although she was expected, Piper left her sleeping bag in the car. If there was no room in the house, she could camp out or find a bed elsewhere. No biggie. Being a restless soul, living on the road was her chosen life. Not because she was unhappy or discontent, merely fiercely independent and filled with the need to wander, explore and paint. The latter, often related by her grandma Thorne in past times, apparently inherited from a well-known and talented artist ancestor.

Which thought always drew out the guilty feelings again, which Piper readily acknowledged but usually managed to quickly douse like campfire coals to stop them spreading out of control.

As always at such family gatherings, she would do her best to ignore the dark glances and stares of unfair accusation, an unforeseen burden she was fated to endure.

As she climbed the back steps, casserole container in hand, Piper breathed deeply, turned the knob and opened the door. Hit with the loud hum of voices and activity, her ebony-eyed gaze flashed swiftly about the open living area to settle on her father. As the oldest bereaved son, it was her duty to go to him first. She set down the casserole in the kitchen, sparing a brief glance of acknowledgement for her mother as she passed, ignoring the other womenfolk gathered there, aware that all attention focused on her arrival. She would speak to them all later.

The cluster of men standing around her father, beers in hand, all respectfully stepped aside for the oldest child, watching the reunion. Jimmy Thorne reached out for his daughter, wrapping her in a long warm hug of welcome. No need for words. Never had been. Piper shared an unspoken bond with this gentle hardworking man.

'You made good time,' he murmured in her ear, allowing her the grace of moments for her quiet sobs to ease.

Until now she had found her grief impossible to express but the mere touch of her father's big arms safely around her unlocked the flood and, as always, he waited patiently for it to subside. When he sensed she was recovered and ready, he slowly pulled away. The surrounding men began to murmur their sympathies to Piper with a nod or touch and she quietly accepted them.

As she left her father's side and moved back across the room toward the kitchen, she darted a side glance. She glared for the shortest moment at her male cousin, Coen, who she had learned from painful experience to mistrust. But she was disappointed and concerned to see her younger impressionable brother, Yarran, in his group.

Piper knew, coward that Coen was, although he may not be directly looking at her, he was beyond aware of her presence in the room. That was enough. Eagle-eyed, the bad seed in the family. The tolerated rebel. She was not really surprised that he was here. Her father would have felt bound to allow it.

If any person stained the family name and reputation, it was Coen. He alone was responsible for Piper's internal struggle each time she returned home, although most people believed otherwise. For Piper, that broken faith in her honesty cut deep and the reason she chose to live away. Because family chose Coen's fake truth over hers. It still rankled that people doubted her word and he had never been accountable for what he had done.

At the time, it had been hers and Coen's word against each other; his convincing distortion of the facts, convenient alibi and coercion of witnesses frustratingly tipping opinions in his favour.

To anyone outside the family, the theft may have been considered merely unfortunate and no particular blame cast. But the rarity and cultural significance of the treasured Thorne family artefact that had disappeared back then lay like a gaping unspoken wound among her mob.

The insinuated responsibility and unjustified accusations on Piper for its loss settled heavily on her shoulders, her innocence unproven. The deception could never be undone. For which she resented Coen and, the way she felt at the moment, could never forgive.

Piper hadn't exactly been shunned by the wider family but living with the fallout and undercurrent afterwards, it had simply been easier to leave, prompted by her suspicion of everyone which had driven her to watch her back ever since.

In the kitchen with low voices, she was embraced among her sisterhood. Her mother Ella, sister Kirra, cousins, especially her favourite Emily, and extended family womenfolk. Fortunately at times like these, the past and assumptions were briefly set aside. At least in her presence. What they said or thought in her absence she neither knew nor cared.

'Welcome home, Piper,' her mother said warmly. 'Thank you for the casserole.'

'From Gracie at the roadhouse.'

'Love that purple streak in your hair,' her

sister Kirra grinned.

'So do I. That's why I did it.'

To her relief, Piper was invited to stay overnight in the cottage with them, grateful to feel part of her family again, at least for a while.

Ella, always critical, couldn't resist adding, 'Would have been nice for you to be here before your grandmother died.'

Accustomed to such reprimands and prickling with irritation, Piper simply said, 'I'm here now.'

Piper often wondered if it was because she was their first born and her parents - well, at least her mother - expected her to shine; set an example for her younger siblings. Perhaps there was also a nibble of disappointment for not being a son. But any hope she may have nurtured, washed away years ago when Piper's character had been suddenly challenged and silently questioned.

Piper accepted a drink and joined Kirra and Emily on the back porch to catch up on gossip.

'You plan on staying down the coast for long?' her sister asked.

'For the winter. It's milder down there by the sea.'

'Yeah, right,' Em chuckled, 'with that freezing wind screaming up from the Antarctic.'

'You still painting?' Kirra persisted.

Piper threw her a tolerant glance and smile. 'Of course.'

'Don't ever stop. You're too talented.'

'Never. Between markets and online sales, I make a good living.'

'Have any friends?'

Being apart from family, Piper appreciated her concern but worried over the anxiety in her sister's voice. 'Sometimes. Casually. I'm not really in a place long enough, you know that.'

'You're not lonely?'

'I don't mind my own company. There's a community of travelling artists out there like me and we keep in touch. Help each other with contacts from place to place. Hey,' Piper nudged her, 'you okay? Where's this coming from?'

'I hate the way you left.'

'I know. But it was my choice and I'm fine with it. Every day brings a new experience and a new perspective. And I might just have a special painting for you. In memory of grandma,' she lowered her voice.

Kirra brightened. 'Now?'

Someone poked their head out the back door and yelled, 'Grub's ready, girls.'

'After dinner.'

Piper rose from her seat, helped her sister to stand and grabbed her tight for a hug. Following a few heartfelt words from Piper's father, everyone filled their paper plates and then spread out on seats both indoors and outside on the front and back porches to share the food and company.

With the mothers tending to Elders and children, the younger girls huddled together again.

'Enough about me,' Piper said. 'What's been happening around here? You still hairdressing, Em?'

She nodded. 'Growing my mobile clients. Like the freedom.'

'I hear what you're saying,' Piper agreed. 'Sis?'

'Still love my secretarial job but sick of living at home. Can't really afford to move out yet though.'

'Anybody you could share with?'

'No one compatible enough. Dad would help but I don't want to ask. As long as I can come and go as I please, I can deal.'

'No boyfriends, you two?' Piper teased.

The girls shared a wicked grin. 'We're doing okay.'

'Be choosy.'

Em groaned. 'We don't have anything to do with Coen's group.'

'Best be not saying his name around here,' Kirra warned. 'Dad's furious our cousin is even in the house and only allowed it because we all know grandma would want it. Mum did some serious talking before he would agree though.'

It hurt Piper to hear that her mother still supported her cousin Coen. 'At least Dad believes in me,' Piper said. 'Mum will always be disappointed.'

'Grandma believed in you.'

Piper sighed and fondly smiled in memory. 'Yeah, she did, didn't she?'

'Me, too,' Em added.

'That's four of us,' Kirra quipped, ever the optimist. 'Yarran's still sitting on the fence but he's easily swayed.'

When the evening grew late, guests gradually said goodnight and left. As Piper hauled her sleeping bag from the car into the house, her father appeared.

'We need to talk,' he murmured, 'but after the funeral.'

'Of course.' Sounded mysterious and she couldn't help but wonder why. Probably just make sure she was doing okay but he already knew that. They kept in regular touch.

After setting up her bedding in Kirra's room on the floor and Piper's long drive up from the coast, the sisters fought to stay awake talking but soon crashed for the night.

Every day until the funeral, native bush flowers appeared from everywhere, arriving at the house or left on the doorstep, since grandma had lived with Jimmy and Ella for many years. There was weeping and hugging, long conversations over cups of tea, memories shared. All a testimony to the widely felt loss of a deeply revered member of their family and community.

Then the day of the ceremonial and spiritual

graveside service arrived. Each family member chose one bright piece of clothing to wear in deference to grandma's wishes, often voiced in her later years, that her passing should be a celebration in gratitude for a long and fruitful life. A true and loved supporter of her people.

As Grandma Thorne was returned to the soil of her country, the family and community mourners grieved and supported each other. For them, the connection between earth and sky was strong and sacred, people and land merging as one. Her spirit would now return to the Dreamtime to be rebirthed as another living creature or part of nature in kinship with the environment.

Confronted by the finality of her grandma's passing and feeling of deep personal emptiness, Piper wept. Kirra clung to her side, the sisters watching their father stoically taking part in every aspect of his mother's ceremony. Emotionally drained by the loss of such a strong family Elder, they all exchanged hugs and tears until the crowd slowly left the cemetery.

Back at the Thorne cottage on the farm, more food and drink appeared, some of the younger men fired up the barbeque but the atmosphere was more subdued now.

Piper ignored Coen again, as though he was nothing more than a ghost among them all, refusing to ever acknowledge him.

Early next morning, Jimmy found Piper.

Rugged up against the winter morning's chill, they jumped in his ute and headed in the direction of Backwater Swamp on the edge of the property. So distant from the house, Piper knew this private conversation must be serious.

Early rains had refreshed the water's higher reaches so that bird life, ducks, black swans and water hens now populated the area.

Her father pulled into one of his favourite fishing spots. 'Come and sit.'

He led her to a log overlooking the calm stretch of water, mirrored with reflections, and they settled together. He removed an envelope from his coat pocket and handed it to her.

'What's this?'

'From your grandmother.'

As she had in life, Piper reflected, her cherished grandma was reaching out from beyond. Touched, she accepted it.

'She gave it to me weeks ago. Before she died, she was working hard on something. Making phone calls, visiting people. Seemed important to her. Figured you might need to read it alone some place. I can go for a walk or come back later.'

Utterly ignorant of what the letter could possibly contain and bewildered, Piper shrugged. 'Did she leave one for the others?'

Jimmy shook his head.

'Then maybe give me ten minutes?'

He rose and wandered away among the

trees around the swamp verges where water birds rustled among the reeds.

Piper looked at the envelope in her hands hesitant to open it, frowning over what could be so important her grandma had felt compelled to reach out to her this way. After a few moments of hesitation, she turned it over, broke the seal and unfolded the sheets of paper.

Piper caught her breath at the sight of the familiar scratchy handwriting. A tribute in itself because her grandma had only learned to read and write later in life.

'Piper,' it began, *'it is time to right the wrong. A copy of this letter has been left with my will at my lawyers so your word will never be questioned again. I leave this information in your capable hands. Paths are made by walking. I know you will succeed.'*

Then followed three pages of the most amazing revelations. Piper's gaze was riveted to every word on every line, her dark eyes wide with astonishment. So much material and research and time invested in its compilation. Clearly driven by her grandma's determined efforts to find enough evidence for Piper to pursue a mission to prove her innocence of the family treasure's loss years before. When Piper had been younger and so much less worldly-wise; wrongly accused of its disappearance.

How on earth had the beloved old woman, despite failing health, managed to leave this inspiring and hopeful legacy?

Piper pressed a hand over her mouth against her sobs but tears freely rolled down her cheeks. Years of private heartache released in a torrent of uplifted emotions. By the time her father returned, Piper was still a mess. At first sight of her through the ute windscreen, his face crumpled with distress.

'Piper?' He opened the door and slid inside behind the wheel again, reaching out his rough tanned hand to cover hers.

Barely able to speak, she shook her head. 'I'll be fine,' she whispered. 'Read this but tell no one.'

He took the pages. When he finished, Jimmy said, 'Now I understand her obsession.' He gazed at his daughter. 'You'll have a challenge ahead to follow up on this. What mother started you need to finish.'

'I can't believe she found a lead.'

'At least you have a place to start, my girl. Good searching.' He paused. 'If you ever need anything, I'm always a phone call away.'

With her grandma's passing, Jimmy alone now knew how much this meant to his daughter. 'I know.'

Even as her father turned the ute around and headed back toward the cottage, Piper already felt changed. Grandma's letter had lit a spark of hope inside her. The fog of her recent past felt like it was slowly lifting.

That night, Piper couldn't sleep. Fired up

with determination, she became excited, anxious and afraid. Not of the task ahead but the kinds of disreputable people she needed to find and outwit in order to be finally free of suspicion and prove her innocence.

For lack of evidence and the nature of the hunt, this was not a cause that could ever involve the law. This was a private family matter.

A formidable thought but she was up for it. She would do everything in her power to make her grandma proud and, in the process, hopefully clear her name.

Chapter 2

Kirra gushed as Piper gifted her the promised painting next morning in her room. 'I love it.'

'A seascape to remind you where I am.'

Then Piper said her goodbyes to family and left later that day. As always, it was the most difficult leaving her father and sister.

Kirra had been crushed she wasn't staying longer.

All Piper could do was offer a scrap of reassurance and leave her with a vague promise. 'I have something I really need to do.'

'How long will it take?'

Piper shook her head. 'No idea. Be back as soon as I can.'

'Keep in touch?'

'Until the cows come home.' Piper was rewarded by Kirra's reluctant smile.

A family joke that had developed in childhood because the animals on Jack's property their father managed included a small milking dairy herd as well as prime beef cattle.

As she drove away from the family cottage alone, Piper knew grandma's information was not only a gift but a huge emotional boost and challenge. Here was a tenuous chance to finally prove her innocence to the suspicious minds in her community.

But first she needed the sanctuary of her favourite private corner and quiet place where she always felt at peace. So she jolted over the paddock track to the far side of Backwater Swamp which in wet years overflowed from the creek east of town. A short distance further around from where she and her father had come yesterday.

Here as a teenager the sights and sounds of nature had first filled her with the seeds of inspiration to combine her own preferred contemporary style of painting yet also draw on the features of indigenous art. Her unique style making her notable among her present day artistic peers.

Piper pulled up overlooking the water, wound down her side window and sat quietly for a moment in her car. The crisp morning air made her shiver and bird sounds, flapping wings and splashing water echoed over the silence.

She stepped out and shrugged on a puffer coat over her hooded windcheater to stand at the swamp edges. With her cold hands sunk deep into her coat pockets, Piper used the surrounding tranquillity to mentally connect with her ancestral spirits.

She gathered strength and peace for the trial ahead and contemplated her game plan. Her grandma's faith and new information would support her endeavour to retrieve the family artefact for its ancestral importance alone. Whereas Coen and his followers had only seen its monetary value.

From time to time over the years, grandma had narrated the artwork's meaning and journey down through the generations. Spoken of its ancestral origins before white men arrived in their land. Entrusted into grandma's privileged possession during her lifetime from her own Elders. If Piper hadn't been so unfortunate and cheated, their grandma would have been able to hand on the rare and irreplaceable treasure to her son, Jimmy.

Piper sank into reflection of the night the artefact disappeared. Permitted to open it, she recalled handling the actual bark artwork, already ancient and fragile. She remembered the feel of it in her hands, its rough texture, feeling reverent in the presence of her mob's treasured history. Its simplicity and meaning had taken her breath away, its rich colours passing beneath grandma's fingers as she traced each symbol, mesmerised by her voice as she explained the significance of its design. As a child and, later, teenager, Piper was awed it had even survived.

Then she had been allowed the privilege of replacing it in its rolled container with tribal markings and return it to its usual safe keeping place, aware that Coen had shadowed her all the way. At the time she thought less of it. He was always creepy. She knew differently now.

By the following day, it was gone. A few days later when the artefact could still not be found, only then, when the community regarded her with suspicion, did Piper realise she had been exploited, betrayed and, in the end, silently blamed.

At the time, she suffered such heartfelt devastation not to be believed. She alone could see her father and grandma were the only people to read the potential truth in a teenager's tear-filled eyes and sobbing voice. At the time, she *had* felt responsible. After all, the artefact had been lost on her watch.

In hindsight, she realised her big mistake was not mentioning Coen's possible involvement to the artwork's suspicious disappearance. He hadn't needed words to threaten. One dark glare from him while she was being questioned by family warned her into silence or consequences would follow.

Her pleas went unheard that she was telling the truth. The very same appeals she now calmly cast out to her ancestors for their help and clemency.

Emerging from the depths of her quiet reflection time, filled with a sense of purpose and calm, Piper knew she might be on the road for weeks and packed her car accordingly. Her backpack was filled ready for a quick getaway if needed. Sleeping bag rolled up. At each step she must have another backup plan in place as an escape strategy. She may need to live in her car and would definitely stay alert. Be smart, out of sight and ahead of the thieves. Well, that was the idea anyway.

This was a contest she could not afford to lose, no matter what it took.

She stocked up on supplies and cash so she didn't leave a paper trail behind. Grudgingly wished she owned a more reliable set of wheels but more importantly kept the old Holden clean and serviced. It had already done some heavy kilometres when she bought it and she was well underway in saving up for a replacement.

For the moment, her second-hand vehicle would have to do. Fortunately, it looked pretty much insignificant which might play to her advantage and suit her purpose down the track. Literally. There was always the possibility she could be hitting some back roads but she had grown up around here in the Wimmera. It was her country and she knew it well. She needed any edge she could get.

Only when Piper considered herself as prepared as possible, not knowing what lay ahead, aware she would face difficulties and need to think on her feet, did she take to the road, driving south into the Western District.

Her destination was a low security country prison to visit an inmate named Denny, suggested by grandma Thorne's missive as the most likely place to start her search.

But first she needed to do some research and prepare.

From her phone, Piper sent off an email to the prison to be placed on Denny's visitor list. When approval finally arrived, she phoned them for a visiting time, scheduled for the following weekend.

Piper checked into a nearby caravan park cabin until the day arrived. Although she was early for her first daunting visit to a prison, there was already a visitor queue waiting to be processed.

Leaving her property at reception, Piper was led into a large room set up with tables and chairs. She took up her designated position to wait, aware of being watched by security officers and cameras.

Shortly after when an inmate appeared and strode directly toward her, Piper knew this was her man. Lanky, reasonable on the eye, although the buzz cut looked rather severe, Denny Marshall paused before sitting opposite.

He scowled with suspicion. 'I don't know you. What's this about?' His voice reflected confidence, deep and smooth.

Where to begin? Since she was operating on limited time, Piper took a deep breath and launched into her pitch. She held Denny's gaze and folded her hands on the table. 'My name is Piper Thorne and I'm looking for a thief.'

He grinned. 'You're sure as hell bound to find heaps in here.' Not said unkindly.

Piper relaxed. She liked his manner and humour. 'A particular thief. My grandma Thorne wrote to you.'

His eyebrows rose and his dark eyes gleamed. 'Yeah.'

'You have information.'

'Yeah.'

'This is a fifteen minute visit. I'm short on time here. Do you have a name, an address? Anything you can share?'

His voice lowered and he leaned forward. 'I heard your grandma is a decent woman.'

'Was. She died last week.' Piper swallowed over the lump in her dry throat. It was the first time she had voiced her passing to anyone and it hurt.

Denny hesitated and muttered. 'Sorry. Listen, I did some digging after she wrote. Contacted some people, made phone calls. Not easy in here you understand?'

Piper nodded.

'I can help you but I need your word. I don't know you.'

'I don't know you either. What you tell me could end up in a wild goose chase.' She stared him down. 'You have my word if I have yours.'

He assessed her at length. 'I'm sticking my neck out here. Word gets back-'

'I promise,' she said firmly.

It took an agonising length of time while Denny processed if she was honest and he could trust her. Maybe a few details would help as ammunition.

'My cousin, Coen Thorne, was involved in stealing something precious belonging to my people and I want it back. Apparently he knew a contact in a small band of local crims and either sold it to one of them or told them about it for a price. Your connection in here maybe?'

Finally Denny seemed persuaded enough to cooperate and nodded. 'Your boy-'

'Coen Thorne is not my boy.' Piper stopped him right there, eyes blazing. 'He's a lowlife who's given our family and community a bad name.'

Denny held up his hands. 'Whoa. Didn't mean nothing. Anyways, Coen,' he emphasised carefully, 'put the word out he had something to sell. The guy in here who bought it must have stashed it. Didn't have time to make a swap because he was arrested soon after. But claims he has a buyer for the piece who's waiting for him to get out soon so they can trade.'

Piper's hopes dropped as she wondered how long that could be. Months? Or even longer.

'Whoever this guy knows, sounds like a big player. Man in here's been bragging about it.'

Denny shook his head. 'Not the brightest spark on the planet.'

Finally, he gave her a name.

'Leo Taylor. He's part of a group I used to know. And trust,' he sneered. 'When he gets out his *mates*,' he stressed, 'will abandon him like they did to me. Set me up. Let me take the fall. Wrong place at the right time for them. Bad for me. I hope you beat them and stop the trade, put a dent in their operation, but I don't like your chances.'

Piper bristled. 'I'm tougher than I look. And determined.'

She knew the odds were stacked against her but she took exception to being considered beaten before she had even started. Her worst nightmare and she refused to accept it.

Denny rose, placed both hands on the table, leaned forward and spoke barely above a whisper. 'Releases walk out the front door early,' he hinted. 'Is nineteen your lucky number?'

Piper caught on. The nineteenth of this month? 'Might be,' she said, working out that was only another week. 'How will I recognise him?'

Denny straightened. 'Twenties, dark curly hair, round face, tallish. Now forget me.'

Piper stood to squarely face him. 'Done, and thanks. How much longer you in for?'

'Two years. Then I'm disappearing. Starting over.'

'Unlike you, I wish you success with *your* plan,' she quipped.

Piper heard his chuckle as she turned and walked out.

Piper was usually restless at the best of times but the week she was forced to wait for Leo's release was torture. Impatient to push on with her search and crack another clue that might lead her closer to her goal, it was a nervous relief when the nineteenth finally arrived.

Soon after daylight, she cruised to a spot in a far corner of the visitor car park outside the prison, hardly having slept the night before. From a distance, she hunkered down to wait.

Within ten minutes another vehicle, black, swept in and took up a place almost opposite the main gate. Its engine rumbled with power and Piper worried if this was her prey, she might have trouble keeping up. She sat up and focused her binoculars. One man. A very likely possibility.

Nervously, she continued to wait. Shortly after eight, a man emerged from the facility. Older and hunched, carrying only a plastic bag of possessions, he walked off alone. Piper relaxed. False alarm. But she grew tense when the next man appeared. Bingo. Exactly as Denny had described. The young man headed straight for the black car, climbed in the back and it sped off.

For Piper, the importance of this moment hit home. Her chase was on. She hastily pulled out and followed the car back onto the main road. It turned left, heading north west toward the highway. With the pale morning sun behind her, Piper kept a distance. The vehicle ahead was sticking to the speed limit. She let other traffic pass so her car wasn't always directly behind and visible in their rear mirror but still within sight.

Piper's tracking of Leo and his mate continued for over an hour. They had joined the main highway and headed for the Wimmera. In one way, reassuring. This was familiar territory but her trouble would be keeping them in her field of vision while staying unrecognised herself.

That difficulty eventuated when the black car slowed ahead and indicated right, leaving the highway for a country side road. Maybe they were heading for a property.

When she approached their turn off, Piper braked and pulled over. The black vehicle was parked in an untidy yard surrounding a rundown timber house.

She pulled in among trees and undergrowth at the roadside, grabbed her binoculars and legged it across the road for a closer look. With no cover here, Piper was forced to hang back, watch and wait.

By dusk, growing cold and after barely a

day in pursuit, Piper soon learned to make friends with patience. Growing stiff and uncomfortable, she debated on returning to her car to spy in comfort until the men each slowly emerged and straggled outside, lit a campfire in the yard and sat around drinking and talking.

In case she missed something important and at least now being blessed with the cover of darkness, Piper crept close enough to hear their conversation.

Sounded like Leo was being challenged by the other man about their deal. 'Where is it?'

Leo laughed. 'So you can ditch me and go get it yourself?'

'You double-crossed me.' His slurred half drunken voice fortunately carried well on the still night air. 'You never met me where we planned. Where did you go after we split up?'

'I told you. I had to hide it before the cops came when I found out I was being nicked for the other business.'

'You were arrested in the mountains.'

Piper frowned and wondered if that was where he stashed the artefact. Is that why they had driven up this way? Crikey, if the artwork was somewhere in the Grampians, they were going to have to narrow it down a bit. The mountain ranges were a National Park on a grand scale and covered hundreds of thousands of hectares.

The men muttered and complained among

themselves. When Piper refocused, she realised Leo was talking again. 'Stop whingeing. We'll head there in the morning. It's down south. All you need to know for now.'

After much shuffling and grumbling, the men staggered to their feet and disappeared inside again. Numb with cold, Piper trusted they would be sleeping off celebrating Leo's freedom and the spoils to come at least until daylight.

She trudged back toward her car, peed in the bush, nibbled on some snacks from her backpack then snuggled under her sleeping bag sitting up in the driver's seat in case she needed a quick getaway tailing the men again in the morning. She set her phone alarm just in case.

Piper woke to the sound of beeping, carefully stretched to flex her aching joints and crunched on a muesli bar and an apple. She wound down a window to hear any sound from across the road at the farmhouse.

A heavy fog had come down so it was almost impossible to see much through the trees even at this close distance.

When Piper heard a car engine burst into life, she scrambled into action, wound up her window and kicked her own vehicle motor over to let it idle and the heater warm up.

Damn. This pea souper would make tailing difficult and dangerous. She'd have to risk staying close enough behind to at least see their red rear lights. Maybe the men weren't as dopey as they sounded and were using the foggy morning to advantage. While it lasted. Being even petty crims, they would no doubt have learned a few tricks of evasion.

As expected, the black car turned north west back onto the highway. But where she would have expected them to turn off at some point and head south along the roads that led into the mountains, they continued until almost back to her home town.

To her annoyance and complete surprise, they left the A8 heading east in the opposite direction to the westerly mountains, and onto an isolated country road. Piper grew concerned. With no cover, she was forced to hang back and follow at a much greater distance. Every now and then while driving, she peered through her binoculars. Tricky to see much while threads of fog still hugged the ground. She grew anxious, feeling exposed and vulnerable.

Then the other car turned left into yet another farm property ahead. Piper jammed on the brakes and parked among trees further back along the gravel road to wait within their shelter, only half hidden but grateful for the remaining light fog.

Piper sighed with frustrated. It was barely midday and she could be here for hours, days. Last night the men had sounded keen to get into the mountains for the artwork, now it seemed like some kind of delay or stalling. What had happened in the meantime? Had they seen her following or grown suspicious and were taking a precaution, or breaking their journey for some other reason?

Something didn't feel right. Piper wrangled with leaving but then she would lose them. So much for all her planning. Useless really, for this on-the-ground surveillance where the situation could change fast. Like now. What to do?

Could there be another road out the back of the farm property? They might already have disappeared. She had the registration number but fat lot of good that would do with no way to identify it.

By late afternoon and an early setting winter sun, Piper decided to risk driving closer to the property and try to spot their vehicle, see if they were still there. At low speed, she crawled closer, keeping watchful both ahead and in the rear-view mirror.

A white car suddenly came from nowhere behind her, eating her up. All she had time to register was that maybe the driver couldn't see her in front of him. If he didn't slow down or stop, she would be rammed.

When the vehicle just kept coming, she grew terrified. Best to get out of the way and let it pass. Piper edged over off the road into the grassy side drain. The approaching car seemed to slow a bit but was still going way too fast and would be seriously close.

As she feared, the car slammed against her old Holden and clipped her close on the right hand front side, giving her enough of a thump to push her all the way down into the drain. The other vehicle didn't stop or turn around, just continued until its dust trail dissolved into the distance.

The collision felt too deliberate and targeted to be an accident. Was this a warning? Had she been seen by the men in the black car? Out here, traffic was light, vehicles infrequent.

Whatever the reason behind the *accident*, Piper's intuition told her she needed to get off this road.

Through all the buzzing thoughts filling her mind, Piper became aware that her right leg was painful and recalled it being slammed against her door from the impact when the other vehicle hit. Her car engine was still running, so she revved the motor and managed to drive up the incline and out of the ditch but could hear the front tyre scraping. Might not be able to travel far unless she checked it out but first she must hide and take stock of her situation.

She wasn't worried about herself, simply angry she had lost the men. Bugger. She thumped the steering wheel with her fist, wondering how on earth she would find them again.

Piper recognised her surroundings. To her right was a thick tree plantation along the fence line of a paddock on private property. There was an access gate and it was near that big old deserted *Banyandah* homestead further along this road.

She nursed and steered her protesting car deep into the shelter of a eucalypt and wattle plantation. Pain shot through her leg as she edged from the car to eye the damage. A decent dent from the crunch around the right front wheel. It would need panel beating to straighten it out to run free of the tyre. Damn. Piper grew annoyed. Only the first day of her surveillance but already she was in trouble. She was hungry, it was almost dark and her quarry was lost.

Piper noticed blood from her wound and her leg ached something fierce. She had been emotionally shocked by the collision but she was ready for this. She pulled her backpack from the car, loaded with basic supplies for just such an emergency, and heaved it over her shoulder. She limped ahead in the dusk toward the open homestead gates and driveway lined with gum trees leading to the old house and possible shelter. She guessed the homestead and outbuildings would be locked. Only when there was no sign of anyone nearby or any lights or vehicles, did she flick on her torch, flashing it ahead as she hobbled and found her way around the dark brooding grandeur of the house to the rear of the property.

A few old sheds and outbuildings loomed

into shadow so Piper accessed one with a broken hinged door and let herself in. She moved right to the back over old piles of timber, hay bales and gardening tools lined up against the walls.

Just when she thought she was safe and could settle for the night, she heard a vehicle arrive and stilled. Visitors. Leo and his mates? It pulled up and the motor died. She shuffled even further back in the shed right into the corner, found some canvas bags and threw them over herself. She heard muffled male voices in the distance then only silence for a long while. Piper didn't dare move or hardly breathe.

Had someone come to check on the property? Rob it? Sometime later, she heard voices again, arguing, before the vehicle started up and drove away.

Piper hadn't realised she was holding her breath until she let it out after they were gone.

Just when she figured she was finally safe and shuffled out from undercover to rummage in her backpack for food, a voice asked, 'Is anyone there?'

Chapter 3

Piper froze when she heard the female voice that sounded right outside the shed. The hinged door slowly creaked ajar. A torch flashed around inside until it landed on her face and she raised a hand to shield the blinding light.

Could her day get any worse?

'Piper Thorne! What on earth are you doing here?'

As her eyes adjusted and she recognised the visitor, Piper relaxed. But she scrambled for words to explain her situation to her former school friend, Addie Kendall.

Stalling for time, she quipped, 'Resting. And hiding, I guess.'

Addie came closer and sat on a hay bale. 'Who from?'

'Can't say.'

'Fair enough.'

Addie was nothing if not reasonable and this wasn't her property either although the Kendall farm joined this one so she wasn't far from home.

'Please don't tell anyone I'm here,' Piper

pleaded.

'Okay.' Addie noticed the blood on her leg and frowned. 'Are you all right?'

'It's not serious. I was deliberately run off the road by another car.'

Addie gasped, horrified. 'That should be reported! Did you get the rego? If you describe the vehicle, we can tell Ewan Holt and he'll trace them.'

'No! I'll be fine in a day or so.'

'Are you in trouble?'

'I've done nothing wrong,' Piper insisted defensively. 'The guy who ran me into the table drain was following, trying to scare me.'

'Why?'

'Thinking I'll give up.'

'On what?'

Piper shook her head and, despite her predicament, managed a twisted grin, deflecting focus enough to say, 'Addie Kendall, honestly, you haven't changed a bit. Talk about twenty questions. All you need to know is that I haven't broken the law and I'm sorting out a family problem.'

'Can I help?'

Piper panicked. 'No. It's complicated. I thought if I hid for a day, it would give my leg a chance to heal. Besides, if the guy comes back, he won't find me or the car. He'll think I've gone.'

'Where's your car now?'

'Hidden in the bush.'

'So it can still be driven?'

Piper nodded. 'But not far. It's been damaged on the side from the crunch. Something's out of whack. Think it's the right front wheel. I knew the homestead was nearby and empty so I decided to rest here until I can move again. Thought I'd be safe and alone until I heard a vehicle.'

'Yes, I saw lights so I came over to investigate. Did you see them?'

'No, I hid here in the shed. Didn't want to be seen or recognised.'

'Only trespassers,' Addie said. 'They've gone now. Being the nearest neighbours, we keep an eye out.'

'I'm surprised the house is still deserted,' Piper said. 'Must be tied up legally since the Ross family was killed and the husband disappeared.'

'Actually I believe the homestead has just been put up for private sale. I guess with all the publicity, the family chose to keep a low profile through the process. You have to wonder who would buy even such a grand homestead like this with its unfortunate history. Listen, Pip,' Addie reverted to Piper's nickname from school, 'I came over on my motorbike. Are you sure you don't want to jump on the back and I'll take you to our place so Mum can take a look at your leg?'

'No!'

Addie must have sensed her desperation

and said quickly, 'Okay but at least let me bring back some first aid supplies to dress that wound.'

'Your mother will know its missing.'

Addie chuckled. 'Trust me, with Mum being a district nurse for decades, her emergency first aid box is loaded. And food,' she added. 'I'll bring back food.'

'Oh, I remember your mother's food.' Piper sighed at the thought of Mrs. Kendall's famous home cooking.

'Yeah, from all those birthday parties on the farm when we were kids.' Addie said. 'I was sorry to hear your grandmother died recently. Is that why you're back?'

In distress, Piper's mind went blank and she could only silently nod.

'I'll be back soon.' Addie promised. 'Actually, do you have a mobile?'

Piper simply nodded again, still upset over the mention of her grandma, the reason behind this crazy chase and her current dilemma.

'Could you keep watch till I get back? Those guys have trespassed before. I've already reported it to Ewan Holt. I don't suppose we could swap phone numbers and if the men return, you could text me?'

Piper hesitated. This conversation was becoming awkward. She had not only lost Leo Taylor's trail but, as always, Addie was being annoyingly nosy.

Seeing her hesitation, Addie jumped in with a reassurance. 'Promise I'll delete you as a contact as soon as you leave.'

Piper believed her and reluctantly agreed so they exchanged numbers and Addie left.

In her friend's absence, Piper took the opportunity to collect her thoughts. The other woman was honest. If she gave her word, Piper could trust her to keep it. She hated accepting help but right now she needed it. Maybe something good would come out of her shitty day after all.

So by the time Addie returned, Piper was in a more positive frame of mind.

Loaded with medical supplies and food, Addie breezed back into the shed. 'Told Mum I was going out to do some night photography, experimenting with time exposure,' she grinned and proceeded to expertly clean and dress Piper's leg wound, securing a covering against infection.

While Piper gratefully tucked into the sandwiches and drank hot tea from the thermos lid, Addie asked, 'How's your family doing?'

'Mother's still as bossy,' she smiled fondly. 'A community Elder now.'

'Ella was always a strong personality.'

Piper shrugged. 'Having a weird mother builds character. She and Jimmy still live out in the rented cottage on Jack's farm.'

'Does your Dad still work for him out

there?'

'Yeah.'

'I see Kirra and Yarran around town when I'm home.' Addie mentioned Piper's sister and brother.

'Yeah. They've both got good jobs.'

Addie hesitated then asked, 'So what have you been doing since you left school?'

'Bummed around for a while. Kinda lost, you know? Then pulled myself together and did an arts diploma for two years.'

'You were always drawing something. Had a natural artist's eye.'

'Yeah. Grandma encouraged me. I travel a lot now and sell my stuff online.'

Addie explained her concern about Piper's vulnerability out here because of the guys who had apparently been trespassing more than once and would probably be back. And with the homestead property being on the market, there would be interested buyers about.

'If you want to stay out of sight,' Addie advised, 'probably not a good idea to stick around so I have a suggestion. Unless you plan on hobbling back to your vehicle and camping out in it, I can set you up tonight at the hollow camp down by the creek on our farm.'

She reassured Piper the Kendalls would keep out of the way. 'This time of year there's no cropping yet so the men won't be about and needing to go into that creek paddock anyway.'

Addie shrugged. 'Think about it and if you agree, text me. I'll set up the camp and return for you tomorrow morning. Now, about your car. If you tell me where it is, I'll get my brother Nick to go check out the damage and fix it.' She chuckled. 'Don't look so alarmed. He's a top mechanic. He'll keep your secret.'

'At this rate,' Piper muttered, 'my location won't be private for long.' Grudgingly, she said, 'It's on the track leading into the nature reserve off Old Creek Road.'

'I know it.'

'It was the only place close with enough shelter to hide a car.'

'Right. I've brought a sleeping bag. It's on the motorbike. I'll go fetch it. You're not going to have a very comfortable night.'

The last of Piper's worries. 'I've slept rough before.'

Addie's generous offer was typical and gave Piper a reprieve. She had been on the road tracking Leo for almost two weeks now. Downside, it meant she would lose a day while her car was fixed. After which, somehow, she needed to pick up Leo Taylor's trail again.

'Thanks for all your help.' Piper sent Addie a meaningful glance. Forced to stop and reflect, she felt compelled to add, 'Sometimes meetings in life, like both of us being here at the homestead at the same time, can't be explained. More than coincidence. Almost mystical.'

'I agree. However it happened or for whatever reason, I'm glad I was around when you needed help.'

After Addie left, Piper reflected again on the fate that had brought them together and sensed the presence of her ancestors. This unexpected hiatus and reconnection with an old school friend was indeed as mysterious as it was welcome.

She dragged two hay bales together, spread out the borrowed sleeping bag on top and snuggled down to catch up on rest.

Piper woke to strips of sunlight slanting across the shed from between cracks in the timber walls. She moved out into the weak morning sun on another hay bale until Addie returned in a battered old farm ute.

'Morning.' Her friend greeted, striding toward her. 'Sleep okay?'

'Fine.'

With a hand at Piper's elbow, Addie helped her into the vehicle.

As they sped along the gravel road to the creek paddock, Addie said, 'Once I've set up camp for you, I'll get a fire going. I've brought eggs and bacon, and a thermos of Mum's soup. Should keep you going today.'

'Thanks,' Piper murmured, looking away out the side window, already deep in thought as to what her next move needed to be. The most likely step made her cringe. But she would examine every other option first. Maybe devise a plan to avoid it.

By the time the tent was up and a fire going, Addie's phone pinged. 'Nick's finished checking your car and he's topped up the fuel tank.'

'That's really generous. I should only need to stay tonight. My leg's not as bad today so I should be fine to drive tomorrow,' Piper apologised.

'No hurry. Stay as long as you need. I'll call back later. You'll be private out here.' Addie gazed around. 'It's one of my favourite spots on the farm.'

After a hearty breakfast and some light exercise, Piper was inclined to agree. She forced herself to do some careful walking down to the creek, following a track along its banks. By midday her injured leg, although bruised and sore, was more flexible and she could almost bear her full weight on it again.

She had also contemplated ideas on how, from her current level of disadvantage in following Leo, to most logically move forward to do something about it.

Since her choices were limited and she finally admitted to herself she would need help in some way, Piper reluctantly conceded there was pretty much only one person she should approach. And it made her sick to her stomach.

Coen.

But she was damned if she would beg and,

ignoring her usual stubbornness and independence, decided on invincible backup so she could face the dreaded meeting with strength and confidence. All it took was one phone call and she was smiling when she hung up.

When Addie returned next day, Piper was already waiting, the tent down and packed away, campfire doused.

'Morning,' her Good Samaritan approached, smiling.

'Great wheels.' Piper indicated her friend's classic old Holden, even an earlier model than her own.

Addie beamed. 'How are you feeling?'

'Better. I won't have any trouble driving.'

'We should get going and it might be an idea to sink low in your seat.' Piper heard the sense of urgency in Addie's voice and then her friend produced and handed over a business card.

Piper looked at it and frowned, noting the man was a private investigator. 'Ben Powell. Name's not familiar. No one I know.'

Addie launched into an explanation. 'Turns out there was plenty of activity last night at the homestead. The trespassers returned. I'd warned the police already so they were staking it out. When they arrested the burglars and searched inside, they found a body in the cellar.'

Piper's mind raced, firstly with horror at the

mention of such a gruesome discovery, and then relief that Addie had wisely removed her from the property.

'I cruised by the front of *Banyandah* this morning on my way here. Police tape and uniforms everywhere. Other cars parked along the road. Reporters maybe. Then a man from one of the vehicles stepped out in front of my car and forced me to stop. Actually,' she reflected a moment, 'I thought he was on the edge of handsome. You know, unshaven, rugged. Cargoes and a black windcheater. Until he suddenly whipped out a photo. Of you, Piper! And flashed it in my face.' She hesitated. 'He asked if I had seen you so I asked if you were in trouble. He just said people were concerned and that they wanted to find you because you might be in danger.'

After the accident, Piper had worked that one out for herself.

'Guy was driving a white SUV,' Addie said.

'Could be the car that ran me off the road,' Piper offered vaguely, scowling. 'Doesn't make sense though. If he's looking for me, he wouldn't ram and leave me, would he? But it was almost dark and I was trying to keep my wheels on the road so I didn't have time for a good look at the vehicle or the driver.'

'Whatever his reason for needing to locate you, he's definitely not on your side so we need to get you way from here. Now,' Addie urged.

'Like I said, police are crawling all over the place.'

'Don't worry,' Piper assured her, 'I'm not wanted by police. Mine is a private family matter.'

Addie looked alarmed. 'I hope all this secrecy and being hunted is worth it.'

Piper had wondered the same thing.

In Addie's car, Piper stayed low, wearing the beanie over her short hair for extra camouflage as they headed back to the reserve where Piper's car was hidden, keeping a sharp lookout for any other vehicles.

As Piper scrambled out and unlocked her car, her friend placed a hamper of food on the back seat. Addie Kendall had gone above and beyond. And believed in her. She wouldn't forget this.

'Thanks for all you've done. I usually don't ask for help,' she confessed.

Addie grinned. 'You have my mobile number. Use it any time.'

'I'll pay you back one day. Somehow,' she promised.

'No need. At some point, we all need to reach out to others.' She hesitated before leaving. 'I hope everything turns out okay for you.'

'Thanks.'

'Keep in touch.'

'If I can.'

'Good luck.'

Piper accepted Addie's quick hug and watched her drive from the sheltered reserve looking both ways before she emerged out onto the road again.

Leaving her alone once more to continue her search.

Chapter 4

Aware she had probably been exposed and was now a target, too, with her vehicle on the opposition's radar, Piper stayed watchful as she cruised to her arranged meeting with her cousin, hopeful it produced the result she needed.

Gilbert was waiting beside his vehicle, beefy arms folded and legs crossed at the ankles.

He straightened as she pulled up alongside him and stepped from her car. 'He's home. I just checked.'

Piper regarded this gentle giant and smiled. If anyone could challenge Coen Thorne and succeed, he could. 'Thanks.'

'What you got yourself into, girlie?'

'You know the gossip. I'm out to right a wrong.'

He opened his car door. 'Ready?'

Piper slid inside. 'I really appreciate this.'

'The kid needs to man up. Today's the day, eh?'

'Coen's going to take one look at you and freak. He respects you. He'll be too terrified to run.'

'I'm one scary dude,' Gilbert chuckled.

'With a heart of gold,' Piper murmured. 'You have another tattoo,' she noticed the delicate heart on his upper arm. She hadn't seen him for months before their grandma's funeral.

'A little token for my angel.'

'How is Leyla?' Piper had been delighted to see her rather swollen belly at the funeral with their first child.

Never big on words, Gilbert smiled and gave a thumbs up, starting the throaty engine. As they rumbled toward their destination, he asked. 'How you wanna play this?'

'Wing it. Carefully,' she advised.

'You got it.'

Piper didn't condone violence but this encounter wouldn't come to that. Apart from looking physically dangerous and intimidating, Gilbert was an honest and revered member of their community. For that reason alone, spineless Coen would stand and listen. And, hopefully, weaken and break.

While his parents both worked, Coen had barely done a decent day's work since leaving school. So it wasn't surprising he was home leaning over the engine of a vehicle that looked like it should be in a wrecker's yard.

Apart from the family dog that barked and raced to greet them, he was alone. But the animal and the deep note of Gilbert's vehicle alerted him to their arrival.

When Coen saw them, recognition and understanding flared across his face. He stiffened like a kangaroo in headlights.

Piper and Gilbert left his vehicle and walked with purpose toward him. Despite his smooth looks and sun browned colouring, Coen Thorne did not look well.

'Too chicken to come alone?' he sneered at Piper.

She ignored him.

'Inside,' Gilbert insisted.

Coen didn't question the demand and they all moved into the house. Piper's aunt kept it immaculate and she always wondered how Coen could be their son when his three older sisters all took after their parents, working full time jobs, taking care of their home.

All three remained standing.

'Where is he?' Piper asked quietly.

Coen's top lip turned nasty. 'Who?'

'Don't play dumb.'

He glared with malice, aware he was ambushed and there was no point in denial. 'Leo Taylor came here and described your car. I told him it was you.'

Piper knew her identity might be discovered at some point but felt doubly betrayed that it was Coen who informed. No surprise there. She hardly expected anything better from him.

'They said they'd find you and deal with you.'

'Clearly they failed. Where are they now?'

'Like I'd tell you.'

Gilbert stepped closer. 'Spill or we get your folks involved. There'll be questions.'

'You don't even know where he is,' Piper deliberately taunted, hoping her challenge to his ego and subtle ridicule worked. 'Leo and his mates would never take you into their confidence. You're not important enough.'

'They came to me for help,' Coen boasted. Pacing. Defensive.

'You're a small fish,' Piper said. 'Leo used you. You're not smart enough to have carried off something like that theft alone. It was their idea. They put you up to it and like the weakling you are, you obeyed them.' She hesitated and sized him up. 'I'll bet you don't even know where he lives.'

'I know exactly where his shack is down south.'

Piper tucked that gem away in her memory while Coen blustered foolish lies that Leo's gang trusted him.

'They even asked me to join them,' he bragged.

Piper chuckled. 'That won't ever happen. Leo undersold you big time on that artwork and now he's going to make a huge profit at your expense. You know our artefact is priceless and I'll bet you handed it over for a song. Easy money that I bet you've already spent. You've been conned, Coen.' Piper grinned. 'So I'll ask you again, if you want payback on Leo and his buyers to show them you're more man than boy, where exactly does he live and where are they going?'

Gilbert had been standing back watching Piper in admiration but he joined the conversation again, pushing closer and looking down on Coen. 'You've hidden long enough, son. Answer the woman and your folks don't need to know.'

Piper shot a glance at Gilbert's declaration, raising her eyebrows in surprise. News to her and not what they had agreed. Then she caught his wink. Somehow she held it together and kept a straight face.

When he hesitated, Gilbert growled, 'Coen!'

The boy reeled back at the sound of their cousin's fierce voice, his expression scared, feet restless. 'All right. Some place down in the Grampians.'

Piper remembered Leo saying something about the southern part of the Grampians. So Coen was probably telling the truth. Thumbs up for Gilbert's threatening physique and support. But she needed more detail.

'The mountains are a big place. You need to be more specific.'

Coen gave a careless shrug. 'Somewhere further south.'

'How far south?' Piper's gaze drilled the boy

until he caved. 'Victoria Valley,' he muttered.

She knew a buzz of promise at the disclosure. A breakthrough for an approximate location. But she kept her cool. Remaining straight-faced, she pushed, 'Do they have weapons?'

'Didn't see any.'

'Still driving the black sedan?'

When he hesitated, Gilbert bellowed, 'Coen!'

The boy nodded, glowering.

While this meeting might have gone down better than she hoped, Piper was not forgetting the small fact that while Leo and his buyer mates had hired someone to run her off the road, thanks to Addie and her brother Nick, they failed to put her out of action. But as a result, she was delayed and twenty-four precious hours behind. She might be chasing a lost cause but she would try.

Piper didn't look at pitiful Coen as they left and certainly had no intention of thanking him. By giving her even the smallest clue, he was simply paying his dues and being accountable for cheating his entire mob years ago.

As they drove away, Gilbert said, 'I'll swing by tonight and tell our aunt and uncle what went down here this morning. With grandma's passing and not being able to hand on that artefact to the next generation of Elders, it's time the truth and facts came out. Although I wouldn't doubt they already have their suspicions.'

Piper madly shook her head. 'It's too soon. Coen may have helped us today but I'm a long way from solving this. I still have no actual proof. It's still Coen's word and mine against each other. Despite what he's told us, he's made no admission of guilt and if he's asked, he'll lie.'

'Can I at least tell them about grandma's letter to you? It expresses her doubt about Coen and her faith in you,' Gilbert said quietly.

'No! I told you that in confidence. Jimmy, you and I are the only ones who know. I want to keep it that way unless I succeed in this search and get the artwork back.'

'All right.' Gilbert shrugged, as they reached her parked car on a bush track. 'I'll keep silent for now. You have my mobile number. Keep me posted.'

Piper nodded. 'Grateful for your help today. If I had confronted Coen alone he would have denied everything and stonewalled me.'

'Sure you don't want me to tag along?' he grinned. 'Some company and muscle might come in handy.'

Piper shook her head and grinned. 'Tempting but you need to stay safe. Leyla needs you. She must be due any day now.'

Big soft Gilbert murmured, 'Sure is. Both just waitin'. What's your plan?'

'Same as before. Wing it. Take one hour at a time. Head south through the mountains and watch my back for a black sedan or a white SUV.'

'Take care, girlie.'

Piper watched her cousin's immaculate powerful machine drive away and felt a pang of loneliness to be on her own again. She had bumbled along okay so far but she had struck it lucky with friends who were there for her when she needed them. One of them, Addie Kendall, by chance.

Flying solo was intimidating and she was fully aware of at least some of the possible dangers ahead. But she would give this challenge her best shot. Grandma would expect it. Her ancestors would expect it. So Piper vowed to do everything in her power to bring the precious artefact home.

Despite what she might have implied to Gilbert, Piper really had no plan whatsoever.

Even though she was close to home, she dared not call in to visit her parents. Only her father shared the knowledge of her secret hunt. Right now, Piper didn't need the hassle of any explanations or questions as to why she was still in the district and hadn't returned to the coast at all. If she told them the real reason and she failed on such an important mission for her people, she would be devastated. So the less people who knew, meant the less people she would disappoint.

For now, heading into the mountains was

about as detailed as her itinerary was likely to get. So as soon as she and Gilbert parted, Piper took back roads across country to the Coach Roadhouse on the highway.

Inside, her gaze slowly trawled the café. No one fitted Addie's description of Ben Powell, diffusing any alarm in her mind, so Piper relaxed. She watched one family leave, all pile into one of the two possible suspect white SUVs parked outside and drive away.

One down, one to go. She was worried for nothing and needed to chill.

Holly was serving meals so Piper grabbed a basket and browsed the small basic supermarket section for non-perishables and checked them out.

Back in the restaurant area, she ordered a salad roll and takeaway coffee from Holly.

'Take a seat for a minute,' the waitress smiled. 'I'll bring it over.'

'Sure.' Piper could see from the line at the counter and mostly occupied tables that the staff had their hands full, the place was buzzing today and that she needed to wait. But she couldn't help feeling edgy. The other white SUV was still parked outside. She would feel safer if it left before she did.

A long five minutes later, Holly finally brought over her drink. 'Sorry for asking you to wait but I need to talk to you.'

From the confidential tone of her voice and

the fact that she sat down when the café was so busy, Piper was instantly wary.

'A guy came in looking for you. Sid and Gracie were in the kitchen so they didn't see him but he showed me your photo.'

Piper's heart sank and she took a deep calming breath. 'When?'

'This morning.'

She hardly dared to ask. 'How long ago?'

'Thirty minutes. Working in this place, you get to know and read people. Especially men asking questions about women. I've made it a habit to be suspicious. Odd thing though, in different circumstances, I might have given the guy the time of day, you know? Had a lazy kind of charm and not too shabby on the eye. But he's a stranger passing through, not a local. Don't worry,' she added hastily, 'the other girls all working today are our usual part timers but I warned them to silence anyway because, unless nosy people show some ID that they're the law, it isn't our policy to give out information.'

'What did you tell him?'

Holly grinned. 'That some people might not want to be found. He left his card on the counter.' She withdrew it from her apron pocket and handed it over. 'I accepted it but walked away.'

Piper took it up and saw at a glance it was the same PI guy, Ben Powell, as Addie had warned her about. 'I'm not in trouble with the law,' she swiftly defended herself.

Holly gently laid a hand on hers and said warmly. 'I know that. I've heard about your artistic talent. Googled you and, I have to say, I'm impressed. Love your work.'

'Thanks.' As always to those who knew her, Piper felt a need to explain. 'I know it doesn't look good but I'm trying to do the right thing for my people and this private investigator is the enemy.'

The guy could still be around. If so, he would have seen her arrive and be waiting till she left. Damn. If he wasn't in here and his vehicle wasn't parked outside, he could be anywhere. Waiting.

As Holly rose from the table and turned to leave, Piper sprang to her feet. 'Did you see him drive away?'

Holly's wry expression said *Are you kidding?* And her eyes flashed around the restaurant. 'Do I look like I had time?'

'Sorry. Thanks for the heads up anyway.'

Holly hesitated. 'If you need any help,' she quickly scrawled on the back of a blank order docket, 'this is my mobile number.'

Piper gratefully took it. Holly only casually knew her but clearly sensed her anxiety. Not knowing her troubles yet extending friendship and offering help without question. She grabbed her salad roll, coffee and grocery bag then walked uneasily out the door.

Powell's eyes could be on her right now. Then two young women chatting madly as they walked past, climbed into the other white SUV and drove away. Piper's legs almost crumbled under her in relief. But having risked even fifteen minutes of her precious time at the roadhouse, had made her impatience return.

From his concealed park at the rear of the roadhouse, Ben Powell smiled to himself. He knew that waitress was too evasive from her reaction after he approached her and started asking questions. One little flicker of recognition in her eyes. She had known something after all.

Good thing he decided to hang around on a hunch. See who turned up. He had learned to bide his time and always got a lead, eventually.

He pressed the starter button on the newly hired silver four wheel drive he had exchanged for the white SUV and settled back into PI mode doing what he loved.

As he watched Piper Thorne walk back to her clapped out old vehicle, he thought how much younger the woman was than he expected. His client had been vague on the phone and hadn't shared too much background but he had a name and a photograph. All he needed. With access to loads of public information, databases and records at his disposal, it wasn't too hard to compile his own detailed profile of a case.

He didn't know why the girl was running or

what she might or might not have done, but he made it a practice not to ask too many questions. Just did his job, whether it was gathering information and evidence or finding someone, made sure he got paid and moved on.

Chapter 5

Light misty rain began to fall so Piper cranked up the heating in the car against the bleak winter day and continued on the highway until the first road sign into the mountains where she turned off and sped into the dense bushland.

She needed to make up time today in pursuit of Leo and his friends but would easily manage it to the southern end of the Grampians by early afternoon. In this soggy weather, if her luck held, maybe Leo and his buddy were lying low; giving her a chance to catch up even if she couldn't locate them again just yet. At least she would be closer. As a bonus, the expansive area was remote and, apart from the village of Dunkeld, was therefore far from crowds. Black sedans and white SUVs should be easier to spot.

So Piper settled back for the drive. She loved the Grampians best in this cold climate, which her people knew as Chinnup, the season of cockatoos, bleak mists and freezing winds. Always more keenly felt in the mountains.

Especially on days like this when the thick bracken undergrowth beneath the towering slender trunks of gum trees revived and glistened with raindrops. Sluggish creeks filled and flowed through winding valleys. The leafy carpet underfoot became slick with moisture while the hilly terrain rang with the sounds of laughing kookaburras and screeching multi coloured parrots as they flashed through the shadowed woodlands.

As Piper munched on the fresh salad roll from the roadhouse, she noticed a silver vehicle slip into view far behind. It looked big enough to be a four wheel drive. As least it wasn't white but her glance constantly flicked into the rear view mirror anyway. Inconsiderate driving without headlights for safety in this inclement weather though.

She decided not to panic and maintained her speed. When the sealed road ended and gave way to gravel, she decided to turn into a familiar bush campground ahead. Wait for the vehicle to pass, just in case, and then resume her journey without pressure. It felt quiet and safe as Piper stepped from her car, shrugged on a raincoat and strolled along a short bush track to the camp toilet.

She emerged to an unwelcome surprise and stopped short. Although they had never met, Piper immediately recognised her fellow visitor. Except he wasn't driving a white SUV but a shiny rain-spattered silver four wheel drive. The same one she had noticed following her moments before. Now parked inconveniently behind her car so she couldn't leave.

Sneaky. Damn.

Holly Duncan had been right though. He was annoyingly attractive, leaning against his vehicle, raindrops in his dark hair, looked like he hadn't shaved for a day or two, his steady gaze tracking her approach. Despite his physical appeal, Piper's body filled with a growing bad feeling. He was a stranger. And they were alone in the bush. Not the best odds. She always knew there would be tricky moments like this so all her senses kicked into alert. She paused at a distance.

'Ms Thorne,' he drawled, his mouth promising a grin.

'Mr. Powell.'

'I just want to talk. I won't hurt you. As you're obviously aware by now, I've been sent to find you.'

'By who?'

'My client's name is confidential. He's concerned for your welfare and wants you found.'

'Of course he does,' she scoffed. 'He wants me off his trail to stop me righting a wrong. As you can see,' she spread her arms wide, 'I'm pretty damn unthreatening and I'm just fine.'

'Ms Thorne-'

'Piper!'

He paused and nodded. 'Piper. My name is

Ben.'

'I know who you are.'

'Great. We're up to speed with each other.'

'Hardly. You're chasing the wrong person. Look mate, apart from the fact I'm getting wet, I don't have time for a cosy little chat.'

'What's the rush?'

'None of your business.'

'I thought country folk were friendly.'

'Not around arrogant private investigators.' She braved a few slow steps closer. 'I have backup.'

'Really?' His voice was loaded with amusement. 'I'd have to challenge that claim because, from my observations so far, you're running solo and it sure doesn't look like it.'

Well, wasn't he just Mr. Efficient. 'You're holding me up.'

He unfolded his casually crossed arms and legs, straightened and shrugged. 'My job is done.'

'Good for you but I haven't finished mine. Move your damn vehicle so I can get on with it.'

Piper edged toward her car. Those liquid brown eyes and that appealing shadow on his chin were part of a package that didn't look particularly aggressive and threatening. He was tall and well-built, would obviously be able to handle himself, where she was slightly shorter and lean but she had a few moves of her own that might surprise and she was ready for him.

'Just need to phone my client and tell him your whereabouts,' he drawled.

Even as he produced a mobile from his pocket, Piper burst out in panic, 'Please don't!' Then felt foolish for suddenly losing her composure in the face of such a cool customer who must have been stalking her for days.

'I have to inform my client,' he said smoothly. 'I'm obligated.'

'Believe me, your *client*,' she emphasised, 'doesn't give a damn about me. Whatever bullshit he fed you, he's lying.' In desperation, when he remained unreadable and seemingly indifferent, she pleaded, 'Please. Don't make that call and let me leave.'

If Piper had been more of a sexy operator, she might have tried female wiles but that wasn't her style. For now, begging would have to do.

'Okay,' he said slowly, after studying her at length in that unruffled manner, his voice softer, 'technically I'm not on the clock anymore and, to be honest, my guy was vague about why he wanted you found. Always makes a PI suspicious and my gut tells me there's more behind this situation.' He waved an arm toward his vehicle. 'I have time to talk. Let's get in out of the rain.'

'I don't know you.' Piper folded her arms, glaring, niggled by an annoying feeling that this Ben Powell just might be genuine but she wasn't yet prepared to give him the benefit of the doubt. 'Why should I trust you?'

'Ditto. But if you're afraid I'll get rough and make off with you, how about you jump into the driver's seat and leave the door open,' he offered. 'Beside the fact I'm personally not that kinda guy, it's not part of my job. I follow and locate people. I'm not the police and I don't have the desire or the power to be heavy handed.'

Shivering with cold now, her usually short spiky hair now saturated and plastered to her head, Piper knew his smooth coaxing could be just a ploy to break down her defences. On the other hand, her usually reliable instinct was having an argument with good sense and logic. Although she hated admitting it to herself, Powell's convincing words had hit home in a comfortable place so she took a leap of faith and grudgingly moved toward his vehicle, climbing in behind the wheel as he suggested. Besides, her wheels were boxed in. She wasn't going anywhere.

He took up the passenger seat as persistent rain gently drummed on the roof. When he reached into the back seat, Piper nervously jerked away at his sudden movement.

Probably aware of the bravado covering her present lack of freedom, he paused for a moment before handing her a small towel. 'For your hair.'

The thoughtful gesture chipped away at

another stone around her defences. 'Thanks,' she muttered, feeling foolish at mistaking his actions as she used the towel he offered.

'For my own reasons,' Ben began, 'believe it or not I do this job to help genuine people. I have no authority to take you anywhere and I'd damn soon lose my licence if I did. I was only hired to locate you.'

Within the sheltered confines of the vehicle, his deep voice lulled her into a dangerous sense of security. That this guy had apparently been tracking her like a hound for days, didn't prove he was trustworthy. Just determined and good at his job.

'You can't force me to go anywhere with you. I'll fight.' Even to Piper's own ears her words of warning sounded weak and ineffective.

'Don't doubt it,' his tone held a hint of that annoying amusement again, 'but even though you look fit, you're hardly an amazon.'

Piper quietly fumed. 'I'm stronger than I look.'

He chuckled low, almost to himself. 'Even knowing you for only ten minutes, that might just be true.' After a pause, he added, 'Give me a reason to forget I found you. Maybe I can even help you.'

Piper glanced across at him in shock. 'Pardon?'

'Tell me your side of this story,' he challenged. 'What's this all about?'

This turn around in the direction of her situation and his stunning offer effectively caught Piper off guard. Ben's unexpected suggestion and apparent willingness to listen created a sliver of opportunity that, right now, she would be a fool not to take. Life didn't always go to plan so, clinging to his enticing proposal, she hoped this wasn't a case of being too good to be true. At this awkward stalemate moment, with Leo and his buddies ahead of her in the chase, what the hell did she have to lose?

That deduction tipped her over to making a reasoned choice. She would tell this guy even if he didn't believe her.

'Promise whatever you say won't go any further,' Ben prompted over her long silence.

Piper certainly hoped so. 'You better not be lying, mate.'

Ben chuckled and said easily, 'You have my word.'

'If you break it, I'll come after you next. I'm getting the hang of this surveillance thing.'

'Good luck trying to find me.'

What an ego! Nothing bothered this guy. She guessed he needed a cool head for his job.

And then, right on top of his downright cheek, he calmly offered, 'If it sits better with you, I can tell you my story first.'

Okay, so he was going to offer up some sob story and get her onside. Be all lies, of course. Nice move. It was dry in his vehicle. A big plus sitting out of the rain. So her earlier sense of urgency had faded with the new development of meeting Ben and not totally disliking the guy.

Be rude not to hear him out. After all he hadn't made his threatened obligatory phone call yet and, clearly, neither of them had any plans for the next little while. Although a nagging anxiety lodged in the back of Piper's mind that she really needed to keep heading south.

But if Ben's own story sounded half genuine and not a pack of lies, she would share her own dilemma. He had offered to help. Maybe he would share some ideas and tactics before they parted, assuming he at least gave her a head start or, best case, left with a promise not to contact his client. Who she would bet anything was the buyer Leo was planning to meet and who had employed Ben to find her to eliminate their competition. Keep her out of the way until their deal was done.

Well, they wouldn't succeed. Their trail might be temporarily cold but she would find them again or not give up until she did.

'All right. Let's hear it.' Piper was drier now, therefore warmer, and feeling generous. 'But no *once upon a times*, okay? Get to the point. I don't have all day.'

The heavier steady rain of earlier that gleamed on the sage coloured leaves of bush foliage, had eased now to a light drizzly mist.

This impasse with Ben Powell needed to be resolved before she could continue. So she was prepared and more than a little interested to listen to what he had to say. But also keen to keep moving on and heading south while there was still daylight to snoop around the bush tracks at the other end of the mountains. Possibly find some sign of Leo Taylor's whereabouts. With every minute she wasted here negotiating with Ben, the trail grew colder.

'I guess it started with my parents' deaths. They died within months of each other. We'd been a close family. I have no siblings so it hit me harder than I expected. I've always been restless. A drifter I guess. Couldn't stomach a desk job. Been backpacking around Australia, getting casual work where I could. Makes a man street smart. Not so much cynical as shrewd.'

Piper noticed he glanced away out his side window as he talked and, from his regretful tone of voice, was clearly already falling into difficult reflection.

'Born to be a PI then, huh?' she offered wryly.

'You'd think.' He pushed out a short laugh. 'I let down my guard. I guess I fell for her in desperation and gratitude. She said and did all the right things so I willingly and blindly scooped her up into my lonely life. We became partners and she moved in to my parents' house with me.'

Sensing what was coming, it occurred to Piper that Ben was a wounded soul, too. For a different reason.

'Only took a matter of months for her to wrap me around her finger. With my complete and foolish participation of course. Then one day while I was at work, she stripped my apartment of pretty much goddam everything of value, including some of my parents' effect in boxes that I hadn't even gone through yet. And disappeared.' He paused and as he turned back to her his jaw clenched with fierce resentment. 'My mother inherited valuable jewellery and my father had always been generous in that department, too, so there was plenty of stuff for the taking.'

Piper could only mentally shake her head in disbelief that Ben's story was eerily similar to her own. Seems they had both been betrayed and burnt.

'I'm so sorry,' was all she could murmur.

'Don't be,' His grin was intoxicating. 'I got angry, hired a private investigator to track her down and recovered most of my stuff. It's not illegal to take back what's rightfully yours.'

'Happy ending then.'

Piper was incredulous and convinced that the woman who deceived Ben must have been crazy to treat him so badly. He seemed like a keeper. She grew uncomfortable at the direction of her thoughts. This guy was supposed to be her enemy.

'After that,' Ben said, 'I thought there must be plenty of other people in the same one-sided situation. Feeling used, helpless. Needing that edge to help them find someone or get answers before they could claim some form of justice or peace of mind and get on with their life. I did my training and qualified for a private security licence and I've been doing it ever since. That was four years ago.'

'Obviously you like it.'

Ben shrugged. 'You need to be curious and have an eye for details,' he said. 'I take lots of photos and videos for evidence. It's usually rewarding but sometimes confronting, depending on what you find. Clients can get worried and stressed. They just need someone to listen and understand.'

A few more pieces of the Ben Powell puzzle clicked into place. 'Like what you're doing for me.'

'More or less. I took on your case but something didn't feel right so I pursued it to see how it played out. Which led me here to you today.' He hesitated. 'Your turn.'

Piper stared out at the soggy bush scenery beyond the vehicle windscreen, admitting to herself that Ben Powell's story appeared to be anchored in fact and she was inclined to believe him. Reluctantly.

Encouraged by his apparent and convincing

credibility, she found the courage to share her own circumstances. A lot was riding on this disclosure. Not only the facts and truth but her roller coaster of emotions and fears from the unwelcome burden she had carried for years.

'My mob have passed down a valuable tribal artefact, probably a hundred years old, from generation to generation. A fragile piece of bark artwork. Its significance and ancestral importance is priceless but some people only see such historic specimens for their dollar value.

'It details in symbols the important milestones and events of the past for my people. With more awareness of our indigenous culture these days, rich collectors are paying significant prices for anything they can acquire. Sometimes illegally. Plenty of greed and ego involved, of course.'

'And this artefact is what you're chasing?'

Piper nodded.

'Why do you need to?'

'As my grandma grew older in recent years, she moved in with my father, her son, and our family. She was a community Elder and the current custodian of the artefact so it came with her and was kept locked in what we believed was a safe place in our house.

'A few years ago we had a large family gathering on the farm property my father manages. As the oldest grandchild at the time, I was allowed to take part in a ceremony where the artwork was released from its cylinder and carefully unrolled so grandma could narrate its story to other Elders, our parents and my cousins of a similar age. Bringing it forward for the next generations. We had all grown up knowing of its existence and importance, and understood it was a special spiritual tradition. A vital part of our mob's folklore.

'At the end of the evening, I could see grandma watching me. She invited me to help her carefully roll up the bark scroll again and stow it back into its tube container. I can only assume I was chosen because grandma was preparing me to one day inherit it from her son, my father Jimmy. It was a great honour.

'Honestly, even back then when I remember that night, my cousin Coen constantly looked daggers at me. Jealousy was written all over his face because he was a male and the same age as me but his father was the second oldest son. I know now he knew what would happen. He had obviously boasted outside our family group about the ceremony and someone had filled his empty mind with the crazy notion of stealing it to make money. Coen has always been easily led.'

Piper paused and sighed, shaking her head. 'My young brother Yarran thinks Coen is an idol. Sure, he has the good looks but has never shown any evidence that he uses his brain or has any motivation to make something of his life. So

I guess for him it was a chance to feel important and exact some kind of pitiful revenge on me. Have the theft blamed on me and my name smeared. Which of course reflected on our whole family.'

'What happened?' Ben prompted quietly over her reflective silence.

Piper frowned in memory. 'I took the cylinder back to its proper place, locked it up, walked straight back to grandma and gave her the key.' She grew agitated as she remembered. 'The whole time I was aware Coen was in the background watching and following me. From the corner of my eye, I could see him being stealthy but not fully revealing himself. I've thought back over those moments a thousand times. After grandma gave me the key it never left my hand until I locked the artwork away again in my father's office. So from that moment until the next day when my father went to check it, the artwork went missing.

'You can't imagine the panic and alarm that followed. Dad grilled me with questions. *Did I definitely lock the safe? Can I remember putting the key in the lock and hearing it click? Did I test the lock afterwards to make sure?* It was never ending.

'Others were questioned too, including Coen. Naturally, he denied having any knowledge of it but you should have seen the smug expression on his face that I was being held responsible. He knew I knew. But there was no way to prove anything. And it's been missing ever since. A massive loss to our community and all fingers pointed in my direction.'

Piper's rising anger flared her mission into a fresh burst of renewed purpose in her heart and mind.

'How did you learn that Leo might have it?' Ben murmured.

Piper smiled to herself. 'Grandma. Maybe as the Elder custodian she felt responsible, although the guilt falls only on the thief. We may never know if it was actually Coen who took it and handed it over, or whether he had some other part to play. Perhaps spying to gather information for whoever eventually took it.

'In the last year or so, apparently grandma must have started seriously looking into what happened. We could all see her health failing so she must have felt some urgency to try and find answers. Even though my father interrogated me mercilessly at the time the art scroll went missing, I knew he and grandma truly believed me. But I was so ashamed, I left home only to realise you can't escape your past. I still carry the stigma of the painting's loss with me and always will. Unless I find it. Slim chance now but grandma found me a lead so I'm not giving up.'

'So how did you find this Leo guy?' Ben asked.

'In a prison actually. Grandma left me a letter with information and a possible source.'

Piper explained, quickly outlining her gaol visit and days of surveillance since Leo's release, culminating in the road accident, two precious days lost in her bush camp recovering and her car repaired with Addie and Nick Kendall's help.

'When I was mobile again after my leg injury, I contacted another cousin, Gilbert, who agreed to team up with me to go and pay a visit to Coen. Leo and his buddies had been in the district on their way from the prison to the mountains so I was convinced he must know something. Gilbert eventually persuaded Coen to talk. All we know from him is that Leo had a shack in the Victoria Valley. That's the slim lead I'm following but he could be anywhere by now.' Piper filled with a pessimistic sense of foreboding that an opportunity had been potentially lost by this delay.

'So we need to get moving then,' Ben said.

'We?'

He raised his dark eyebrows and said firmly, 'I'm offering to help.'

Chapter 6

Piper knew it was a good thing she was seated or she might have fallen down in shock. One moment Ben Powell is chasing her down, the next he's suggesting they team up!

'Does this mean you're not phoning your client with my whereabouts?'

'Not yet.'

'You still don't believe me!' she accused, frustrated that *her* honesty had not been accepted at face value. 'I believed *your* story. What if I had said it was a load of rubbish just to get my sympathy? How would you feel?'

'Sure. I get it. No spite intended. Let's both take a step back here,' Ben suggested easily, half raising both hands in a gesture of concession.

Mad with disappointment and unable to shake a feeling of being played, Piper managed to keep her mouth shut for a few moments and reset her mind.

'Will you hear me out while I make a suggestion?' Ben asked quietly.

Now he was being reasonable? 'Make it snappy. If you're not turning me in – yet,' she pointed our wryly, 'I need to make tracks.'

It was still early afternoon and the dark clouds above the trees were thinning, making the day brighter even if the sun wasn't shining.

'I can do snappy. My private investigator's licence allows me access to loads of services. Do you have anything on this guy Leo at all?'

Piper shrugged, hiding her kick of interest at the mention of his resources, a glimmer of promise softening her strain. 'I can give you a physical description of him and the men he's travelling with. They're driving a black sedan.'

'Make and model? Rego?'

'You can find all that out?'

'Yep.'

Piper gasped. 'Random. I have the licence plate written down in my car.'

She scrambled from the four wheel drive and almost stumbled in her haste to go grab her folder. So much for staying cool at how much Ben could contribute to her search. Moments later, she returned and gave him the information. In her absence, he had produced a laptop which was open and ready to work.

With a few key strokes and scowling in concentration, he said, 'Okay, so the vehicle is a BMW registered to a Vincent Minetti. City address. A classy set of wheels so either the guy himself has money or his backer sure does. This kind of operation takes planning and muscle.'

'So you think there's an even bigger fish

buyer behind this?'

Ben shrugged, frowning at his laptop screen. 'Starting to look like it. In these situations, I've learned where there's money there's power. We'll need to tread carefully but, in my opinion, Leo and Vince don't sound like they quite fit that mould.'

'Makes sense,' Piper jumped in, 'because when I followed them to the farmhouse the first night Leo was released from prison, I overheard them talking around the fire and they seemed like followers not leaders.'

'My bet is they're working for the meal ticket.' He cast a long steady glance at Piper. 'That ancestral artwork must be worth a bundle if the big guy has waited years to get his hands on it and employed middle men to help make it happen.'

Overwhelmed and bewildered by such instant promising progress, and all because of Ben doing his job and finding her, Piper asked, 'So what's happening here? What are we doing?'

'We're teaming up.'

'We are?'

'If you agree.'

'We're on the same side now?'

'Accidental allies,' he grinned.

'What about your client?'

'On the backburner for now. I'm holding up my final judgement but, from what you've told me, I'd say he hardly told me the full story.'

Feeling happy and smug, Piper said, 'So is there something you want to say to me?'

Ben flashed her a wary half smile. 'I took this job to find you in good faith. Clients sometimes forget to share important details. Ignorance or deliberate, you decide. Happens more often than you might think. PIs adapt as we go. So how about, for now, we both focus on finding the same guy we're after?'

Piper was torn between the appeal of Ben Powell and the fact that, until half an hour ago, she had been his target. Drawing on her instinct to pull up a huge leap of faith, challenging his loaded gaze, she eventually added, 'Okay.'

A situation that now meant sharing close quarters night and day for the immediate future with a guy who, thirty minutes ago, had been an enemy and a stranger.

'We'll only need one vehicle. Makes sense to take mine, right?'

'Nothing wrong with a classic Holden,' Piper defended with spirit.

'Except speed.'

'True,' she grunted.

'Best not to leave it out here in a national park. If a Ranger finds it and no owner, could look suspicious. They'll trace the rego back to you. Your family might be alarmed if the authorities get in touch and believe you're missing or,' he paused, 'worse.'

'I'll text my dad.'

'Okay but since our return date's open at this point, how about you drive your car into Halls Gap and we leave it in a more public place?'

Piper nodded. 'Makes sense. You're not afraid I'll take off and disappear?' She couldn't resist the tease.

'In those wheels? You'd be lucky.'

Ben eased himself from the passenger seat and Piper followed his lead.

'I'll meet you in the Gap,' he said as they crossed paths in the front of his vehicle.

As Piper climbed into her car and tapped out a quick text to her father, she marvelled at the swift change of events the last hour had brought into her life. She began to focus on the possibility that with Ben Powell's knowledge and moral support, of all people, she had a real chance of finding Leo and Vince. Who they both hoped might lead them straight to the artefact and their mystery buyer.

Her mood lifted as she pulled out of the bush car park and turned out onto the main gravelled road in the direction of the Grampian's main tourist village.

Despite her early fear and misgivings of the guy, Ben's outwardly sincere personality conveyed trust. He had information and skills her own amateur efforts could never match. And, apart from her father and grandma, he was only the third person she had entrusted with her truth of the unfortunate past event that had led to this current situation.

With an improvement in the weather and this new positive development in her search, the drive through the damp dripping native forest seemed shorter and her prospects for a successful mission now at much better odds.

Entering the winding road into Halls Gap, hemmed in by soaring mountains either side, Piper chose a visible but less used car park away from the single main street. Ben's four wheel drive slid in beside her soon after and he helped transfer her belongings, reshuffling his own basic gear in the boot with meticulous organisation.

Piper locked her vehicle but when she headed around to the passenger side of Ben's four wheel drive, he stopped her.

'Tell you what, I guess you know these district back roads well?'

'Sure.'

'How about you drive?' He dangled his keys in front of her. 'I'll keep working on my laptop. See what else we can learn about our mates on the way.' When Piper hesitated in surprise, he added, 'Sound like a plan?'

'This is a rental. I'm not an authorised driver.'

Ben shrugged and drawled, 'You're a country woman. I'm sure you can handle it.'

'Not this fancy. My normal is old Holdens

and farm utes.'

'Promise I won't tell a soul.'

Piper had always loved pushing boundaries. Kept life exciting, so she snatched the keys. 'Be my pleasure.'

Ben climbed in beside her, buckled up his seat belt and opened his laptop again. He tossed her a lazy grin as she settled in behind the wheel. 'You ready for this?'

'Let's find out.'

As Piper cruised the powerful four wheel drive down the central mountain valley tourist road that snaked between the impressive ridges of upthrust sandstone, she grew excited with expectation. Together, she and Ben could do this. She *would* recover the artwork so central to her mob's history.

'It's only 65 kilometres to Dunkeld but because it's a winding route, it should take about 45 minutes.'

'Right,' Ben replied in a focused trance, still staring at his laptop screen.

'Any leads?'

'Yeah. Both guys have heaps of form. Minor stuff though. They're either dumb lucky or they know how to bypass the rules. Just checking now on property title holdings in the Victoria Valley. See if anything matches up.'

'Your work sure is different.'

Ben spared her a considered glance. 'Can be.' He rubbed his palms across his eyes and stretched.

'Do you usually get asked to find or follow people?'

'Mostly. The two main methods of gathering information are plain old surveillance and circumstantial evidence.'

'How do you know where to start?'

He shrugged. 'Name, address and photo from my client. Stakeouts. Plenty of waiting and watching. Learning people's movements. If I need to tail on foot, I follow from the left hand side because most people look over their right shoulder. If I have a good enough reason, I can put a GPS tracker underneath a vehicle. So once we hit civilisation again in Dunkeld,' his gaze scanned the surrounding mountains and occasional bush track that led off the main road, 'let's keep our eyes peeled for that black BMW.'

Piper nodded and sighed. 'We should get that lucky.'

Ben dropped his attention back to his laptop research. As the kilometres sped beneath their tyres, Piper admitted that within a matter of hours since meeting this man, he had become an unlikely ally. Yet, although they had both warily revealed parts of themselves, she also felt he was far from being a friend and still an unknown.

It was a weird sensation to be drawn to another human being and yet cautious with unanswered questions and misgivings. Like, why was he *really* helping? What if Powell was operating to his own agenda and benefit? Was that smooth quiet charm and casual air, a trick and strategic approach to gain her confidence?

If so, it was a good move and working just fine with her but she would be watching her back every moment.

Driving into Dunkeld, overshadowed by the spectacular backdrop of two smaller mountain peaks, Ben closed his laptop and said, 'We need to stay alert now.'

'What do you suggest?'

'Our guys will need the same as us. Supplies, fuel. They know you but not me. Maybe I should drive, scope out the streets and you sit low in the back.'

Piper slowed and pulled off the roadside before they entered the town. They made the changeover and Ben cruised slowly into the village along the main street, covered by all the usual basic small community shops and services. A café on one side and general store on the other where most cars were parked. But no black BMW.

They found an old bakery in a side street, travellers would be spoiled for choice in a variety of holiday cabins and cottages, not to mention the rather impressive upmarket Royal Mail Hotel.

Piper noticed Ben constantly glancing out the side windows and in the rear view mirror. At first, she flattered herself believing, for whatever reason, he was looking at her until she realised he was being super vigilant.

Get a grip, she told herself. *This is business.* 'Haven't been here in a while,' she said.

'We best organise a bed for the night then grab some food and keep out of sight. We can't take any chances.'

With the afternoon light fading, the chill crispness of another approaching winter evening stung the air. Nestled among mountain shadows, night dropped early here. Having camped in her car lately, Piper was definitely on board with the heartening idea of actually having a roof overhead, at least for one night.

'I notice you brought a sleeping bag,' Ben continued. 'You okay with bunking in a cabin together?'

'Sure.'

Ben toured around until he found likely accommodation with a vacancy. He left the vehicle and disappeared into the office, returning moments later with a key. 'Two bedroom cabin, bathroom and a wood fire. I asked for the one furthest back from the road in the bush for privacy. After we unload, I'll go grab takeaways.'

For the first time since meeting her former adversary, the full impact of their close quarter situation sank in. So after they hauled their bags inside and Ben drove off to find some eats, Piper quickly indulged in her first long hot shower for days and changed into fresh cargoes and a hoodie. She washed her smalls and hung them in her room, shutting the door behind her.

When she returned to the cosy living area, the fire had spread its warmth. Darkness had fallen outside so, as a precaution, she drew the curtains first before turning on some lights. Her stomach growled. It had been a long but surprising and productive afternoon since her salad roll lunch.

The crunch of tyres on gravel and flash of headlights outside signalled Ben's return. His gaze lingered over her when he stepped inside. Maybe she looked less feral and more civilised now her short spiky hair with its purple streak was freshly washed. She hadn't even run a comb through. Just ruffled it with her fingers as usual. All the same, he was definitely checking her out.

Finally, Ben broke his gaze, holding up the large promising paper bag he carried, releasing tempting smells. 'Hope you like burgers and fries.'

'Not fussy. Just hungry.'

As a distraction so they weren't looking at each other, Piper filled a kettle and set it to boil. Ben spread out their food on the small table and they sat in awkward silence for a while as they ate. When the kettle boiled, she sprang up and poured hot drinks.

Because the cabin was so quiet, although Ben appeared comfortable enough, Piper felt the need to make conversation. 'So you live in Melbourne?'

He nodded as he finished a mouthful. 'In my parents' house. Well, it's mine now.'

'Being a man of freedom, how's the city working out for you?'

'Not good but it's where most people live so that's where the jobs are. How about you? Where's home for you since you left your family?'

'Not one place. On the road.'

'Damn straight?' He sounded fascinated.

'Yeah.' Piper hesitated. Having finished her burger, she fiddled with folding the used wrapper. 'I paint.'

'An artist?'

She shrugged. 'Guess it's in the blood. Grandma encouraged my talent. I stay places for a few months then move on. Sell my stuff online. Before my grandma's funeral and this search, I was living down on the south coast.'

'Going back there?'

'I guess. Eventually.'

Silence fell between them again for a short time until Ben said, 'About this trip, we should start heading into the Victoria Valley first thing tomorrow.'

'Absolutely.'

Ben fished a map from his pocket, pushed aside the remains of their meal and spread it out on the table, glancing across at her from time to time as he spoke. 'So I guess we go back to the main road from town where we came in and head north along here?' A finger of his sun-browned hand trailed the C217.

Piper nodded. 'Plenty of district side roads branch off. We should check every one as we go. Needle in a haystack,' she sighed, 'but we need to start somewhere.'

'If we work it methodically we can cover plenty of ground. Any buildings or vehicles we investigate closer. See anyone, we ask questions.'

'Make it easier if we knew where to look.'

'Don't be discouraged,' he said softly, tossing her an encouraging grin. 'According to this map, there's an airfield deeper in the mountains.'

'Yeah, probably about an hour from here.'

'I suggest we go there first and work our way back.'

Piper frowned. 'Why? What's wrong with searching all the country in-between as we go?'

'Instinct. I'm thinking any bigwig buyer with money, assuming he's likely to live in Melbourne, just might drop in by air. He won't waste four to five hours on the road. He'll consider his time valuable. If he's a passionate collector, he'll want to inspect the goods for himself. Our guys won't get paid until he has it in his hands and is satisfied. The man might even bring along a professional expert to authenticate the piece.'

Piper stared at him with respect. 'You've done this before.'

Although less then twenty-four hours ago she thought otherwise of Ben Powell on first sight because he stood in the way of getting what she wanted, Piper was now more than pleased to have him on her side. She hoped. Else why was he being so diligent on her behalf? Sure, he wanted to see where his original client fitted into all this but his approach seemed genuine and he was serious about his work.

Ben eyed her steadily. 'My money's on the airfield. You be willing to camp out in winter in a stakeout?'

Piper slowly released a sound something between a sigh and a moan. 'In a good cause, right?'

'We'll be living by the hour,' he emphasised.

'I know. I've been doing it for a while already.'

'Of course,' he acknowledged.

Initially, Piper had planned to do that anyway but certainly not with such depth of experience and the measure of muscle that Ben brought to their challenge.

'That a yes?'

She smiled as she gave a nod.

'We pack up each morning and see where the day takes us.'

'Got it.'

Ben rose from the table, folded up the map

again and slid it into the side pocket of his backpack. Noticing Piper's look of intrigue, he explained, 'Hard copy in case there's no mobile reception for GPS. Get a good sleep. Next few nights don't look too promising for comfort.'

'I'll clean up here,' Piper offered. 'I've used the bathroom so it's all yours.'

'Noticed. Thanks.' He paused, turning back before leaving the room. 'See you in the morning.'

'Night,' she said absently, making herself busy in the kitchenette, avoiding looking at him again which she was finding increasingly fascinating.

Piper tried to stay positive about the days ahead, despite knowing she had lost a vital day after her road accident. Even if Leo and his mates had waited out the rain for just a few hours, that lessened the distance between them with a chance to catch up.

Despite that disadvantage, Piper just knew they were close. She couldn't explain why but sensed it and prayed the artefact hadn't been recovered and sold yet.

Ben was canny to suggest targeting the airfield. His logic and strategy were sound and might just put them back in the game tomorrow. At least there were strong odds that both sides of this struggle were all in the same area now. That thought alone punched up her enthusiasm.

Chapter 7

Piper's sleep was cosy but restless. So she woke early to bird sounds, the rustling of nature's creatures in the damp undergrowth and the sight of kangaroos grazing virtually outside their cabin door.

With no sign of Ben yet, she stoked up the fire, added more wood and went out onto the front porch. Weak sunlight glowed on the eastern sides of tree trunks. After the rain, the soggy eucalyptus bush released its minty scent that drifted all around. Piper rubbed her arms and inhaled deeply.

'All alone?'

Piper jumped as Ben appeared silently beside her, hair rumpled, feet bare. Looked like they had both slept in their clothes.

'Not anymore,' she said dryly.

'We should pack up, grab breakfast and food to go for a few days then hit the track.'

Piper smiled, 'Organised so early.' Deflecting the sight of Ben's trademark calm focused expression and that softness governing his mouth, she turned inside, enjoying her last moments of warmth and civilisation for who knew how long?

All business out at the car later, Ben said, 'I'll drive. Since this is your territory, you navigate. Okay?'

'Sure. I have dried soup and snacks in my backpack.'

'Me too. We'll pool our supplies,' he murmured. 'When we're not in the car, we should keep our packs on at all times. Never know when we need to make a run for it. Be prepared for hiccups,' he shrugged. 'We'll be in the area for a day or two. Depending on circumstances, we can make a quick trip back into town here if necessary. But we should stay out of sight as much as possible.'

'Of course.'

Thankfully the café and general store were already open. Piper gave Ben her order but stayed in the vehicle while he went inside. Learning from his habits yesterday, she kept vigilant until he returned, not recognising any person or vehicle. The locals didn't give more than a cursory glance toward a pair of few winter tourists who braved the region this cold time of year.

Ben seemed to take ages in the café and Piper noticed he ducked into the general store as well. Must have forgotten something.

'All clear?' he asked when he eventually returned, sliding behind the wheel again.

'Seems to be. Pretty quiet.'

Although Piper would have given anything for a glimpse of a certain familiar black sedan to suddenly appear. They needed to find it and the occupants before the artwork was sold and disappeared forever. Now they were on the trail, the importance of success only intensified in Piper's mind.

As they headed onto the Victoria Valley road further north into the mountains toward their airfield destination, Piper enjoyed her breakfast burger and coffee with packets of sandwiches already in a cooler bag for snacks during the day ahead and possibly tomorrow. If Leo didn't show.

Meanwhile, the scenery was as beautiful as she remembered. The farmlands and grasslands were sunlit with mountain peaks a stunning backdrop. As usual, Ben's glances constantly flicked about. He seemed edgier this morning.

After a while, he drawled, 'We might have a slight problem.'

Piper checked her side mirror. A vehicle was following at a distance. 'It's not black. This early probably a local.'

'We don't trust anyone. Next road on your GPS that shows a track off here that eventually leads north, let me know.'

Piper pinched the screen with her fingers to zoom in for a likely detour. 'There's a road left ahead a few kilometres, goes off in a loop and back to this one further on. A few others do the same thing.'

'Okay, we'll stop at that next corner. Get the rego when the vehicle passes. And keep your head down.'

'What if they stop?'

'I'll ask for opposite directions to where we're going.'

At the intersection, Ben pulled over and Piper sank just low enough in her seat to still see the number plate while he pretended to scowl at his phone. The following vehicle slowed, Ben waved as if all was okay, the other driver waved back but both the male driver and his passenger were strangers.

'Get the licence?'

Piper nodded. 'Are we okay?' she asked as the vehicle grew smaller in the distance.

Ben shook his head. 'Looks innocent enough. I never feel right taking chances. They followed us since town.'

He turned down the side road until he found the shelter of roadside gum trees a few kilometres further on. Ben scrambled out and knelt on the ground, looking under their vehicle. When Piper walked around to his side, she heard him curse.

'What's wrong?' she said to his legs and feet. The rest of him was half underneath the four wheel drive.

'We've been tracked.' Ben emerged with a

device in his hand. 'Must have done it overnight. How the hell did they identify us?'

He found a large rock in the grass and smashed the tracker. He paced back up onto the road. 'We need to find another set of wheels.' Hands on hips, Ben gazed at Piper with raised eyebrows. 'Ever ridden a motorbike?'

'I grew up on a farm.'

'Brilliant. Drive back to town like your life depends on it while I check that number plate.' He grabbed and opened up his laptop.

'If they're trailing us, that's good, right?' Piper asked. 'Means they're still in the area and they probably haven't handed over the artwork yet. If the transaction was done those guys would be gone.'

'You're right. But if they were Leo's spotters, they know we're here, our description and that there's two of us. If they are working for the other side and that information is passed onto the guy who hired me, I'll be identified and they'll know we're working together. Otherwise I would have already reported locating you.'

'Should have,' she corrected. 'And only if I was recognised as your passenger. Otherwise they might still think you're tracking me toward them, right?'

Ben shrugged. 'Possible but let's not push our luck, huh? This is a serious operation and it has one determined buyer who won't let anyone stop the deal. At least we know we're on the right track. They're in defence mode and alert to us now. So we need to ditch this vehicle fast and hire us some bikes.'

As Piper sped back into Dunkeld, she couldn't stem the nerves and building urgency churning inside her stomach. 'We could also be wasting time and lose them again.'

Ben shook his head. 'Don't panic. I removed the tracker. They found us in the valley but they have no idea we were heading for the airfield. That's why I pretended to be checking a map, looking like we might be lost or scouting the area. I understand how you feel but what we need now is a clear head. This move will save us time in the long run and put us at an advantage.' He hesitated, frowning at his laptop screen. 'Rego is coming up as being for hire. Half of the companies are illegal operators. They swap plates between vehicles. Drivers are often not registered so not police checked and they don't get pulled over by the highway patrol. Smells like Hendry. We'll add it to our watch list.'

As they entered the town, he said, 'Pull in to the garage up ahead on the right. They'll be able to hold this vehicle and point us in the direction of some bikes. This is a farming community. They'll be everywhere. Bikes are easier to hide and can go off-road where other vehicles can't.'

Piper stopped and Ben disappeared inside. She accepted his reasoning and forced herself to trust his judgement, hoping this delay took the smallest amount of time so they could get back into the valley and their destination. The airfield. At least they were anonymous again and not being tracked. Which meant secrecy, the upper hand in finding their targets and up close surveillance. So long as they remained undetected.

Bursting with a sense of nervous energy, Piper stepped from the vehicle and paced outside the garage, watching Ben calmly chatting to the mechanic like they had all day to spare. She wished she had his outward cool and patience. Then the men moved out of sight and, a short time later, Piper heard thunderous revving from somewhere out the back.

Cripes, if that was their new ride, Leo and his mate would hear them coming.

Within ten minutes, Ben returned grinning. If the previous noise was any indication, he had acquired something, which meant travelling very light and no cover from the winter weather.

'You should have heard that thing,' he gushed.

'I did. Isn't there anything quieter?'

'Don't worry, Pete's changing the muffler. She'll purr.'

'Cats purr. Motor bikes rumble.'

Ben chuckled and rested a hand on her shoulder. 'Not this one. Trust me. Now, grab all the food you can and stuff it in your backpack. I'll put my small tent, tools and gear in mine.

There's only one set of wheels so we'll be riding double. Pete's parking our vehicle out the back till we return. Paid extra for him to throw a cover over it and keep our transaction private. Old guy was tickled when I told him my job. He took a copy of my PI and driver's licences but he'll keep our details private.'

'All that in twenty minutes. I'm impressed.'

'When the muffler's silenced, he'll fuel up the bike and bring it around front. We'll lose less than an hour.' Ben couldn't keep the delight off his face. 'Wait till you see that machine. No one's catching us on that baby.'

'Sounds dangerous. Should I be worried?'

'Not if you're up for a few thrills.'

The challenge made Piper both excited and afraid. Not exactly what she had expected from this mission but, hey, since Ben bailed her up in that bush car park, her luck had turned around big time. She wouldn't argue with her fortunate turn of events.

The mechanic appeared from around the rear of the garage wheeling the *machine*. To Piper it was all sleek lines, black and chrome with a slash of red. According to Ben, the kind of bike with enough grunt to escape their worst enemy. She hoped so. They may need it.

It was a long time since she'd ridden on one. They would be physically exposed to the elements and far less concealed than in a vehicle but for flexibility, she guessed it would work.

After Ben introduced the guy as Pete, and Piper as his business partner, they shook hands. Then Pete handed them leather jackets and full face helmets. Fitted out, Ben shook hands with their mechanic, they shrugged on their backpacks and legged it over the bike.

When Ben kicked over the motor, Piper felt the power and vibration beneath but not the roar she expected. Whatever Pete did to the muffler, it worked.

Ben half turned to her and said, 'Hang on.' Then they were off.

Once Piper found her footing and balance, both arms wrapped tightly around Ben's waist, she began to enjoy the experience. Wearing helmets, they would be anonymous to any other traffic.

Once out of town and on the valley road again, Ben revved up and they took off. He maintained a steady cruising speed through farming country between mountain ranges.

All the time Piper was aware of the closeness their travelling situation created, crushed together on the bike. Not unpleasant but increased the level of intimacy Ben must be feeling too with a female plastered against his back.

The striking views continued to impress as they entered Mirranatwa Gap, passing an art studio surrounded by a neat corrugated building and gardens. Piper would have loved to stop but, if her memory was right, they were about halfway to the airfield and on a mission so it was no time for sightseeing.

Soon they were heading deeper into the heart of the craggy mountains and thickening eucalypt forest. It hit Piper that, had she pushed on alone in her search, the loneliness of the area would have seemed daunting, dark and hemmed in as they were now by this isolated backcountry.

With hand signals, Piper directed Ben until she heard and felt him reduce speed as they left the sealed road and turned onto gravel. The airbase gate, anchored by sturdy timber posts either side, loomed ahead. With no fence, they easily slipped around the partial barricade at one side and slowly motored along until the bush opened up, revealing a stretch of grassland that formed a rough airfield runway with outbuildings across the other side.

A smaller high shed with aerials was set above another. Clearly a communication and observation tower of some kind. Ben stopped the bike but the airfield was obviously deserted. As the engine idled beneath them, he pointed toward the far end of the field which Piper presumed would give them cover as they approached.

Creeping forward with caution, Ben skirted the perimeter keeping behind the tree line and pulled up near the airfield buildings. After almost an hour on the bike, for Piper it was a relief to dismount and stretch her legs.

Ben removed his helmet and hung it on the bike then immediately began to stride out scouting the whole area, trudging through the surrounding bush, testing all the locks on the building doors and peering in the few small windows.

'It's still early,' he said. 'If they were going to do the deal, it would be while they still have plenty of daylight. While we wait, I say we make camp further into the bush.' He glanced behind. 'Far enough from the sheds where there's likely to be action but close enough to stay hidden and keep watch.'

They moved the bike to a likely spot, offloaded their backpacks and Ben pitched his small tent behind undergrowth.

'Isn't it premature to be erecting that?'

'It's shelter, and disposable if we need to leave in a hurry.'

Piper idly wondered how they would both fit in it tonight if they needed to stay. Promised to be a squeeze. It wouldn't provide much warmth but, as Ben said, it would at least be some protection. Sleeping bags should deal with most of the chill of a winter night in the mountains.

The remainder of the morning and early afternoon proved uneventful. Piper and Ben took turns keeping the binoculars trained on the track in from the main road and, from time to time, scouted together further afield through the bush for any sign of a possible opposition hidden camp like their own, but found nothing.

By late afternoon, as light faded with the sun sinking behind the mountains, a brisk dampness settled in the air. Kangaroos and emus emerged from cover for their evening graze over the airstrip.

'No plane's going to land today,' Ben murmured.

When he began gathering firewood, Piper said, 'Won't that be risky?'

'Not for any chance of a bushfire. We'll keep it small and built in a circle of stones so it's easily doused if company arrives.'

'Fair enough, but I was thinking of being seen. If Leo and his mate ever show up,' Piper added in doubtful exasperation.

Ben gave a low chuckle and the amused reaction filled her with warmth. He glanced out to where shadows were already creeping across the grassy airfield runway. 'No chance of that tonight.'

He was so sure. Piper hated to be a wet blanket all the time. She was fed up with waiting but her grandma's determination to find out more about their people's lost artwork had left her a valuable legacy. It was now her obligation to follow up on the lead and try to get it back.

Growing frustrated by inaction and to keep

herself busy, she helped gather more wood and small rocks. Ben soon had a small fire going and filled a billy from a rainwater tank by one of the bigger buildings. The hum of its heating, the only sound imposing on the crisp biting edge in the air ahead of approaching darkness.

They shared yet more sandwiches and snacks, washed down with a reviving mug of hot bush tea. No longer hungry and partly thawed by the campfire's glowing coals, Piper managed to relax, feeling more agreeable than earlier.

She privately called on the spirits of her ancestors for a sense of peace, and belief that her mission with Ben proved successful. The ache deep inside her for that seemingly unreachable hope left her feeling drained and vulnerable.

'Seems odd having an airfield in the thick of mountains,' Ben murmured from where he sat on the other side of the fire.

'But necessary for easy evacuation in bushfires and emergencies. Helicopter access as a firebombing base. This whole mountain region is a major tourist attraction. Companies offer flights in and out for businessmen and travellers.' Piper reflected a moment. 'We all use this country but don't own it. We belong to it. One indigenous site in this area dates back over twenty thousand years. Puts our country into perspective since white settlement only happened 130 years ago.'

Across the low flickering flames, Ben's steady brooding expression and eyebrows slightly dipped above his gaze, settled on Piper. She caught her breath at its intensity.

'Incredible.' His response was barely audible. 'We don't fully appreciate how old our country really is.'

'My ancestors walked this land,' she said softly and proud. 'They know when you walk through.' And she drew strength from that. On a sudden thought, she asked, 'Why did you really decide to help me?'

Ben considered her again for a long time. 'What you told me raised suspicions in my mind about my client's motives. My job is all about people. Dealing with them. Tracking them. Finding them.' He paused. 'You're one of the good ones.'

He should tell that to her family. Piper's heart filled with humility at his words, especially coming from a man she barely knew but was slowly getting to know and trust. But while Ben remained chilled and confident, Piper still couldn't shake a restless fear and voiced it.

'What if they've already been and gone and we've missed them.' She rubbed her arms and stared into the fire, reluctant to meet his gaze because it meant she doubted his decision.

Despite the change of topic, Ben would know exactly what she meant. After a short silence, she braved a glance in his direction. He rose and moved around the fire beside her.

Hunkered down, their bulky leather jackets brushing against each other, he drawled, 'I know it's asking a lot of you but please stick it out with me. I've learned to work with my hunches and they rarely let me down.' Without barely taking a breath, he went on, 'You know I'd really love to see some of your artwork.'

Piper rolled her eyes and tossed him a knowing glance.

'See what I did there?' he grinned. 'I'm serious.'

'Not just a distraction?' she challenged.

Ben shrugged but wasn't drawn to respond. Knowing him as much as she did with a streak of dogged persistence that had not only located her but served them well since becoming a team, if she refused, Piper guessed he would only nag. So she drew out her mobile phone and flicked through her photos, settling on a few specimens of her work to show him.

He appeared to be absorbed while he took his time viewing them. 'You're quite a talent,' he said eventually. 'You use outback colours. I love how you incorporate indigenous design into modern.'

'Thanks.'

Ben's compliment was genuine. Somehow it seemed important that he should appreciate and understand their meaning. Piper pocketed her phone again as Ben stood up.

'We should get some sleep,' he said. 'It could be all on tomorrow.'

'We can hope.'

Piper hesitated, eyeing off the tiny tent and wondering how comfortable she would feel crammed up against Ben inside it.

Perhaps her hesitation drew his attention because he murmured, 'It's a one-man really. Tonight that will be one-woman. I'll bunk down out here. Keep an eye on the fire and an ear out for any callers. Can't imagine they'd come here at night but it never hurts to be ready. I'd rather not be surprised.'

Piper tried to hide her relief. 'Are you sure?'

He nodded. 'I'll wake you if there's any action.'

Piper crawled into the tent, reluctantly removed her leather jacket because it would be too bulky for sleeping and unrolled her sleeping bag. Zipped up and snuggled inside, the sharp wintry night air still bit. She wriggled around to get more comfortable, listening to Ben moving about outside. Piper was used to roughing it. Her roving lifestyle virtually guaranteed it. She only hoped her current purpose for discomfort and trouble proved worthwhile.

At some point, as she mulled over the day's events, the anticipation and fear over her mission and the unexpected appearance of an enemy who had become a valuable ally in the last forty-eight hours, Piper must have fallen asleep.

She woke to pale light filtering into the tent and Ben softly talking to someone. She tensed and set up. When she warily peered outside it was to witness his one-sided chat with kangaroos emerging from the bush for their early morning feed. Three or four big greys were close to their camp perimeter, sitting high on their back legs, head turned in their direction, eyes alert, long ears pricked.

Piper knew sudden movement would frighten them away, besides this was their territory, so she sat cross-legged in the tent opening and quietly watched. Ben soon became aware of her presence, turned and smiled.

A billy already simmered and sang on the coals, and their snacks were dwindling so breakfast would be light. Dried soup in a mug and nut bars.

'Sleep okay?' Piper murmured, stretching, shrugging back into the cosy warmth of her leather jacket again and moving closer to Ben by the fire.

'Good enough.'

Ben's facial growth had darkened over the two days they had travelled together. It suited him. Gave him an air of rugged mystery. Piper wasn't much for clean shaven and suits. She knew people with beards, tattoos and earrings so the sight was nothing new. The bushman look sat well on him.

The roos had gradually lost interest in their human intruders, loped away into the bush and disappeared. Ben and Piper shared their meagre rations.

'A thick steak would go down well,' he said, sipping thin soup.

'Oh, don't,' Piper groaned.

Ben chuckled. 'If the guys don't show this morning, it will mean another night out here. We need to keep up our strength and nip back into town for more food supplies.'

'We can't both leave,' Piper said. 'We might miss them.'

'I agree. One of us has to stay.' At her questioning glance, he said, 'I probably have a better chance of dealing with a couple guys. Or avoiding them in the bush. If necessary.' He casually shrugged to ease Piper's alarmed expression.

'How we can possibly grab the artwork even if we see it?' Impossible to keep tension from her voice.

'We have absolutely no idea how this will all go down. We have no choice but to wing it. Seize a moment. Create a distraction.'

'What kind of distraction?' she asked dubiously.

'We'll know it when we see it.'

Piper shook her head. 'This is *not* sounding good.'

'As soon as you're ready, we'll do a recon of

the whole area. See what stuff lying around might be useful or a place that might potentially provide an opportunity.'

So they cased out all the sheds and outbuildings again.

'Can we pick the locks?' Piper suggested. 'See what's inside.'

'Good idea in theory or an emergency but Leo and his mate would notice a break in and be alerted someone is around. If he's in touch with Hendry, the finger will be pointed directly at us. We need to keep our presence a surprise and do our best to get the better of them, preferably while they're making the trade.'

'I'm a runner. I'm fit.'

'Great. Thought you looked wiry and supple,' he teased. 'I have two strong arms. Together we'll make a threatening team.' Was he kidding? 'Once we see the artwork, it will be a last minute snap decision. We'll need to move fast and leave. The bike should give us an advantage if we need to head off road to escape.'

They waited tediously through the morning hours, doing patrols to the edge of the bush where they hid, ears constantly strained for the sound of a vehicle echoing through the bush on the approach road, or the drone of a plane engine, or beat of chopper blades.

Piper was troubled and fed up with waiting, hopelessly addicted to fearing the worst because, in her opinion, it didn't sit easily to have no sighting of Leo and his mates. With every passing moment her anxiety grew.

Frankly, she would give anything right now just to hear voices or see a vehicle or any kind of aircraft so she knew they had been wise to follow Ben's lead and suggestion. That the deal for their family's artwork wasn't already done and the crooks long gone.

Beyond midday after another hot mug of tea and the last of their food, with no sight of a plane or vehicle at the airfield, Ben caught Piper's worried expression.

'I'd say they're lying low until they get the nod for the trade from their buyer.'

'You don't think it's unusual we saw a suspect vehicle yesterday and today they're a no-show?'

'Not really, but any action probably won't happen today.'

Piper sighed. 'You said that yesterday.'

He reached out and gently laid a hand on her arm. 'Don't be despondent. I'm used to this waiting game. Our time is getting closer. Listen, I think you can safely head into town for supplies.'

Piper panicked at the thought of leaving Ben, becoming separated. Anything could happen to either of them while they were apart. But they needed to eat. Hunger made you weak. Damn Leo for this delay. And she still couldn't ditch the thought he and his mates could be celebrating his success while she and Ben waited in vain.

'Any food requests?' Piper asked shrugging on her backpack.

Ben crossed his arms and shook his head. 'Cash, not credit card.'

She nodded as she strapped on her helmet, legged it over the bike and kicked it into life, testing out the controls.

'She's an easy handle.' Ben raised his voice to be heard over the engine. 'Enjoy the ride.'

Chapter 8

More than once, Piper was almost tempted to slow the motorbike, turn around and head back to Ben at the airfield. The constant doubt that they had chosen the most sensible action, nagged at the edges of her mind. Spoiling what should have been the thrill and joy of a carefree breezy ride.

Too late now. The decision was long made and they had no choice but to follow through. Ben was right about one thing though. The awesome machine handled smoothly. Mindful she was out in the open and exposed, Piper kept flicking glances in her side mirror for anyone trailing but there was little traffic on the road.

She just needed to focus, get more food and return as soon as possible. Glancing up at the mountains with the sun's light already only a glow behind the highest peaks, it seemed likely she might be returning at the earliest in dusk or by headlight after dark.

Although reasonably disguised on the bike in leathers and head hidden under a helmet, Piper still cruised warily into Dunkeld. Her gaze flashed side to side along the main street. She felt watched and uncomfortably visible as she parked and removed her helmet. Her face and identity now open to view.

In one way, Piper hoped Leo and his mates weren't around in case she was recognised. Yet on the other, also madly wished they were. She would risk discovery in order to end this unbearable waiting game. If she saw them first, she could race back to warn Ben.

In this cold weather, it was no problem keeping food for a day or two. God forbid their stakeout should last longer. So she grabbed fried chicken, yet more sandwiches and fruit from the café along with more protein bars, judging it was more than enough to fill her backpack and their stomachs.

Piper darted quick glances in both directions before she emerged out onto the street again. She was about to don her helmet at the motorbike when a familiar female caught her eye across the street. As the woman stepped from a sporty blue vehicle and glanced about, Piper thought she recognised a school friend. At least she was convinced it was Billie Gibbs but wasn't sure until their gazes locked.

It *was* Billie. She would know that self-assured figure anywhere.

From a distance, they acknowledged each other with a guarded smile. Piper waved, Billie gave a slight nod. Both hesitated, mutually reluctant to take the identity further.

Who knew Billie's reason for the uncertainty but Piper was driven by an urgency to return to Ben. On a random impulse she thought *Stuff it. I went to school with her. I can spare five minutes to be polite.* So she was the one to take the first steps, casually striding toward her former classmate across the road.

Billie stood beside her car, unsmiling, forced to wait and not looking particularly happy. Although as she drew closer, Piper gauged it wasn't because of her approach but an overall sadness of expression and visible mood. As though at the least there was something on her mind or she had just received bad news.

Piper didn't recall Billie being so serious. She always used to be up for fun. And, if she remembered correctly, was friends with Addie Kendall. What were the odds of meeting two of her old school friends within weeks of each other after years of moving on and losing touch?

'Hey, Billie. Been a while. What brings you to the mountains?'

Billie sent her a challenging stare. 'Do I need a reason?'

A surprised Piper started at the blunt response and shrugged. 'Unless you live here now, I guess you're travelling through.' She tried to ignore the lack of welcome and aimed for pleasant.

'Taking a break,' Billie said evenly. 'I can

work remotely.'

'Not really a holiday then I guess, is it?'

Oddly, Billie missed the humour, her expression cool, and Piper scrambled for conversation until her friend said, 'We're all connected these days wherever we go, aren't we?'

Sounded like a brush off but was pretty damn true. She and Ben relied on his satellite phone in their isolated situation, grateful that if they met danger or injury, they were in touch with the outside world.

Encouraged by her friend's small effort, Piper asked, 'So, are you staying or moving on?'

For the first time since they met again, Billie's temperament softened. 'Depends. I'd forgotten how refreshing the Grampians are in cold weather.'

Billie's responses all sounded rather vague. But then confronted in her own situation hiding in the homestead shed when Addie Kendall found her, Piper knew the feeling of needing to keep her reasons secret. Perhaps Billie was in a similar awkward circumstance of her own.

Piper remembered that Billie and Addie Kendall used to be close friends. Always in friendly competition with each other being the maths and computer whizz kids of the class. Piper wondered if they kept in touch.

'I ran into Addie Kendall when I was home recently.'

Billie barely acknowledged mention of Addie and didn't seem particularly interested in the news. 'Haven't seen her in years. You don't live in Horsham anymore either?'

'No.' Considering her present situation, Piper felt reason to be evasive herself with no need to explain. 'I came back for my grandma's funeral.' Which had triggered a whole bunch of stuff she was still dealing with. She really must get back to Ben.

Billie's brow dipped into a genuine frown of concern. 'Sorry,' she murmured. 'So what brings *you* to the mountains in the middle of winter?'

'Kind of a detour on my way back down to the coast.' Piper moved the focus of conversation away from herself. 'You heading home then to see your folks?' she probed.

Billie glanced around. 'Possibly.'

That sounded odd in itself. Who returns to their home town and doesn't visit the parents?

'Be staying at a friend's place out of town by Reedy Lake.'

Piper didn't recall any houses out that way. Just one or two pretty basic fishing huts.

'I might hang around another day or so,' Billie went on. 'Wind down. Take things slow.'

Sounded like Billie had been under some kind of pressure recently. 'Yeah. Life can be like that. Well, if you stay, there's plenty of accommodation. We stayed at bush cabins. Comfortable and cosy.'

'You're travelling with someone?'

Oops. She had fallen into that one. 'Ah, yes. A friend.'

Billie regarded her a moment longer then said, 'Well, nice to run into you, Piper. Say hi to your *friend*.' Her mouth twitched with humour. 'Might see you around.'

'I doubt it. We're camping in the bush. Just came in for supplies.'

Later, as Piper rode the motorbike back along the valley road toward the airfield, she passed the art studio cottage again. Its warm lights within glowed softly out into the descending evening. Piper felt an awareness of connection to the cold winter season and this land. Comforted by a blanket of peace that her ancestors silently watched, sending Piper a sense of their spirit. Reminding her she was never alone.

Closer to the airfield, where the forest thickened, the sun had long since sunk behind the mountains. Only thin shafts of waning light filtered through the trees.

Cautious as she rode closer to their camp, she slowed, idling along with less engine noise before she stopped. No vehicles in sight yet. Although she hadn't expected any. But she played it safe anyway. Just in case.

At her approach, Ben rose from where he was hunkered down by the camp fire. He greeted her with warm appreciation as she handed over the welcome food bags.

Since the encounter with Billie in Dunkeld was casual enough, Piper mentioned it as they sat cross-legged together in the gloomy dusk, hungrily demolishing the chicken and fresh bread rolls in their fingers.

Ben didn't seem concerned so she briefly related their conversation. 'Billie was a good friend of Addie Kendall. You know, the girl who helped me after I was run off the road when I was trailing Leo? She lives on a farm nearby.'

Ben nodded, his mouth full, licking his fingers.

'It really is a small world to see Billie and Addie again after not seeing them for years,' Piper reflected.

Later, they hugged mugs of hot tea by the fire, satisfied after a decent meal. Ben had dragged out Piper's sleeping bag and cosily draped it around her shoulders for extra warmth.

'Thanks,' she murmured at his thoughtful gesture.

'On such a calm night, if anyone comes, we'll hear them,' Ben said.

The glowing coals pushed out heat and light toward the shadows of surrounding bush. This moment of quiet companionship was rare. Since meeting up, she and Ben were continually figuring out their next move or trying to make headway in the chase.

He was growing on her and she found herself watching him in guarded silence. The easy demeanour. Likeable nature. Undeniable attraction. At least on her part. On occasion, she caught Ben's private glances in her direction. Maybe he was just checking on her but it certainly felt like *more*.

He was the ultimate organiser. Always had equipment within reach. Night vision binoculars, camera, flashlight. Not to mention their vital satellite phone link to the outside world.

Early next morning, Piper woke to Ben leaning over her in the tent, a light steadying hand on her shoulder beneath the sleeping bag. He placed a finger to his mouth signalling silence. She nodded.

His warm breath tickled her ear as he whispered urgently, 'Today.'

Piper knew what that meant. Afraid yet excited, having been convinced they had missed Leo, she almost cried with relief. All she could think of now was how they could possibly get their hands on the artwork. Neither she nor Ben had discussed any ideas or strategy. Depending on the situation how that might happen. At least they were in the right place after all with a chance at its recovery.

Ben pointed to outside the tent, his backpack on and signalled Piper to do the same. As she shrugged it on, Ben crawled out first and Piper followed. The silent bush of the previous night had been replaced by the sound of vehicle engines and voices that echoed to them through the otherwise calm chilly air.

'They've just arrived.' Ben whispered. 'The deal is on.'

'We don't have a plan.'

'We can only play this one move at a time,' he reassured her. 'Keep watching. Pick our moment.'

Piper noticed the black BMW had returned with Leo and Vince, a four wheel drive Range Rover parked alongside carrying two new men. One tall, the other short and stocky.

Ben pointed to the taller new arrival. His gaze narrowed and his mouth set. 'My client, Hendry.'

Piper nodded and murmured, 'He was in on it then? Leo must have warned him about me.'

Ben's expression remained steely. She could only imagine what was on his mind right now. He must feel used, yet vindicated in at least hearing Piper's story. Going with that gut instinct, believing, and taking her side.

While three of the men loitered, the short one climbed the outside stairs up to the communication tower. Clearly preparing for the arrival of a plane.

They crept closer, Piper scanning the surroundings, hoping to sight any kind of tube she might recognise that held the artwork scroll.

It could be in one of the vehicles or hidden elsewhere. She presumed it would be in a safe place but how near or far from here was anyone's guess.

Hidden behind the biggest shed where the vehicles were parked, Ben and Piper occasionally and cautiously risked a glance beyond. One man cut the shed padlock on the door, roughly shoved it open and could be heard rummaging around inside.

Piper took a moment to silently send out thoughts to her grandma and all the ancestor spirits who had gone before. Feeling the weight of the expectations, their reliance on her to get back the precious artefact that had belonged to her people for generations.

Finally, action, when Hendry jumped into the four wheel drive and headed across to the grassy runway where he patrolled, chasing kangaroos and emus off the landing strip. Ben and Piper amused at his antics, waving his arms out the windows and yelling to scatter the grazing wildlife.

While he was at a distance and the shorter man up in the communication shed overlooking the airfield, Ben and Piper were close enough to eavesdrop on Leo and Vince in low secretive conversation.

'You should get the goods,' Vince muttered unhappily.

'Not till the last minute,' Leo growled. 'And

I'm going alone. I don't trust any of you.'

'How far away is it?'

'None of your business.'

'When's the buyer arriving?'

'As soon as Eddie gets word on the radio.'

Vince shook his head. 'You should be leaving soon, man. In case of problems. The big guy won't like waiting.'

'When I'm ready.' Leo snapped.

'Lot of money at stake here. Better know what you're doing.'

'No rush. I know exactly what I'm doing and how long it's gonna take.'

From the nearby high shed, Ben and Piper heard a radio crackle into life but not Eddie's short reply.

He emerged and descended the ladder. 'One hour,' he told Leo and Vinnie.

When Eddie wandered off to light a cigarette, Leo pulled Vince aside, leading him by the arm further away into the bush. Looking behind to make sure they weren't followed. At that distance, neither of the two new arrivals could see or hear them.

Ben and Piper shared a glance. Interesting. Out of sight and keeping low, they crept parallel alongside, treading carefully. Watching where they put their feet against a twig crunching under their boots, exposing their presence. And the risk of being caught before they found what they were after.

When Leo and Vince were apparently far enough away, Leo said, 'When I'm ready to leave, make sure I'm not followed.'

'Sure, man. You gotta dig it up in the bush?'

Leo nervously shook his head. 'If they double cross me and something happens, you need to know where it is, okay? Go get it and sell it to someone else. You tell no one, understand?'

Piper thought Leo's reasoning sounded flawed. A moment ago he had said he didn't trust anyone, now this? Her hearing sharpened but, just when she thought she would learn the relic's hiding place, Leo's voice dropped. She strained to hear the rest of their exchange, but thought she heard something like *echo*.

'Way up there?' Vince exclaimed.

'Not so loud, you idiot. You know it?' Vince nodded. 'Right. You watch my back, man. Promise?'

'Damn straight.'

'We only know about this because that Coen kid blabbed. This is just between you and me, right?'

Vince nodded. The two men turned and loped away toward the buildings again.

Piper's heart almost stopped after Leo and Vince left. Surely not! Could it be that easy?

In a lightbulb moment, she nudged Ben, beckoning and dragging him away to follow her back into the bush toward the motorbike.

In an urgent whisper, Piper said excitedly, 'I

think I know where the artefact might be hidden.'

Chapter 9

'We went with your hunch about the airfield as a potential meeting place, right?' Piper said eagerly. Ben nodded. 'Now I have the same instinct about where the artefact might be hidden.

'I'm positive Leo said the word *echo*. That triggered a memory when my cousins and our families came down here camping. Us kids used to scramble up the rocky paths and slopes in the area. Among them, we climbed up to what we knew as the Echo Cave. It works,' she said wryly. 'We tested it at the top of our lungs. Our voices carried over this whole valley.

'Anyway,' Piper went on, 'it makes sense now that they chose this airfield if Leo hid the artefact nearby. I wonder if that was Leo's suggestion. Coen said he had a shack around here somewhere, right? What do you think?'

'It's a long shot and we lose valuable time if it's a fizzer.'

'I know. It's a bit of a climb but might be worth the risk. If we leave now to check it out, we could get ahead of Leo. He hasn't left yet because the little guy hasn't gone back up to the communication shed. We could be up to the cave and back within the hour. Before their buyer flies in.'

Ben looked back through the bush toward the airfield, frowning over Piper's suggestion. 'Okay. Let's give it a red hot try.' Piper beamed. With a restraining hand on her arm, he added, 'But we're gonna have to push the bike far enough away so there's less chance they'll hear it when we start it up.'

'We just need to go back around the top of the airfield to the other side where the track comes in from the main road. Another trail branches off into the base of the mountain. A path leads up to the cave.'

'If any of the men hear us, they'll be in their vehicles and across the airfield straight onto the road. Good chance they'll either catch up to us or catch us, full stop.'

Piper's anxious gaze locked onto his. 'Mad idea?'

'Hell, we've been playing hunches for days. Let's go.'

Piper sent out a silent plea to her ancestors to watch out for them as they raced to the bike and pulled on their helmets. With Piper up front steering the handlebars and Ben pushing the vehicle from behind, they jogged away from the airfield buildings and back around through the bush at the top end of the runway.

Even then, knowing it was still a risk, Ben kicked the engine into life, Piper leapt on behind and they chugged away at slow speed. Keeping to the cover of the bushy undergrowth and gum trees, Piper kept looking back across to the airfield buildings to see if anyone had heard their motor. So far it didn't look like any of the men had been alerted to any sound. The vehicles were still parked in the same place.

Ben kept weaving among the trees, directed by Piper. Eventually, they came across the trail in from the airfield track road and turned onto it, pushing closer to the mountain foothills.

They were now far enough away not to be seen so Ben opened up the motorbike and they sped along the overgrown winding track to the bottom of the cliff face following it around until Piper indicated to stop.

As they dismounted and removed their helmets, Ben asked, 'Is this the only way in and out?'

Piper nodded.

Ben shrugged. 'So if we meet Leo on the way down?'

She grinned. 'There's only one of him and two of us. We have moves. Stick with me. I'll look after you.'

Ben slowly shook his head, amusement on his face. His intense covering gaze flipped and warmed Piper's stomach.

Knowing the way, she led, always climbing,

sometimes more easily along a winding rocky path, others scrambling over boulders, at times leaping across water gushing over them after the recent rain.

Ten minutes later, stopping for the first time to catch their breath, Ben quipped, 'Leo was no fool to stash it up here.'

'And we have no idea where it's hidden when we get there. If it's even here at all. There are heaps of nooks and crannies. If we don't find it, maybe we can wait and ambush Leo when he arrives.'

'Let's keep going and worry about that when we get there.' He glanced back over his shoulder to the valley below and airfield beyond. 'The vehicles and men are still there.'

Five minutes later they were taking deep steps up the rocks, then over a short stretch of damp sand and small stones, gaping up in awe at what lay just above them. The wide opening overhang of Echo Cave.

Climbing into it, Piper and Ben stood together, hands on hips, spreading their gaze over this marvel of nature, a mammoth cool chamber. Slivers of water glinted on smooth rocks and the sounds of dripping from above echoed all around.

'It's huge,' Ben said. 'Lots of places to look.' He eyed the fissures and crevices, all likely places to hide an old artwork.

'You take that side,' Piper indicated to their

right, 'and I'll take this one.'

They each retrieved a torch from their backpacks and began the hunt. Pressed by a sense of urgency, they worked in silence far longer than Piper's anxiety could endure. She ran her hands over even the smallest crack in the walls and peered carefully, terrified to miss what they were seeking.

After a time, as they moved closer back toward each other, Ben said, 'There are hand stencils here.'

'Yeah. Most are found in rock overhangs because that's where my ancestors would have sheltered. Up here is a strategic viewing point.' Not that they had the time to look and appreciate it yet. 'There are hundreds of rock art sites in the Grampians dating back twenty thousand years but only a handful are open to the public.'

Eyeing the dampness and water in the cave, Ben said, 'I hope Leo wrapped up the treasure well against the elements.'

'Knowing the money involved, he wouldn't have taken any chances. It will be someplace safe and dry.' When she and Ben met in the centre of the cave after they completed their first scouting without success, Piper said, 'Damn the man. We'll need to work further back in the cave.'

As they moved deeper into the narrow cave reaches, slowly and carefully lighting up and probing into even the smallest possible fractures and possible hiding places in the rocks, valuable minutes ticked by. Piper really had to work her mind to stay positive and not be overwhelmed by frustration.

'What if we don't find it,' she said quietly, almost to herself, yet knowing Ben was listening nearby. 'It might not even be here.'

'Keep looking,' he said with a quiet reassuring calmness that stimulated Piper to push on.

Deep in concentration, her thoughts wandering and elsewhere as they continued to search, Piper heard Ben grunt and rustling. She froze. No way! She closed her eyes, sensing Ben beside her.

Afraid to look, she hesitated then spun around, gasped and pressed both hands over her face. Ben held the familiar roll in his open palms wrapped in a scrap of uneven leather in thick protective plastic. Leo had taken good care of it. But then he would. He intended making a lot of money out of this fragile relic. She couldn't believe her eyes were actually seeing what she had dreamed about for years and hunted for weeks.

'We didn't!'

A few wayward tears escaped and rolled over her face. Piper's first thoughts were for her grandma; that she could now proudly hold up her head before her people with its return. Which would not have been possible without the letter leading her on a possible new course. It broke her heart that grandma would never see this but she strongly believed, somehow, somewhere, she would *know*.

Piper felt the gentle touch of Ben's hand on her leather bike jacket sleeve. 'We need to head back down. How about you go out to the edge of the cave, make sure all's quiet down at the airfield while I stow this safely in my backpack.'

Speechless with a bundle of emotions, Piper nodded and stepped down from the cave. All seemed well below. When she glanced back, Ben was still rummaging in his backpack. What was taking him so long? Clearly he was making sure the artefact was secure.

When Ben finally joined her again, they set off, their descent faster, because it was easier although dangerous and aware they were racing against time and the enemy. All went well until they were about halfway down, no longer level with the treetops, surrounded by thick undergrowth.

Piper abruptly pulled up, raising a hand for Ben behind her to do the same. 'Do you hear a vehicle?'

After a second's hesitation to listen, he nodded. 'Leo's on his way.'

'Damn. I wonder how close. He'll see our bike!'

Piper began running as fast as the track would allow, skimming over boulders, Ben breathing heavily close behind. If they could just make it back to the motorbike before Leo…

The moment they reached the bottom of the cave track, Piper knew they were sunk. The four wheel drive from the airfield was parked behind their motorbike, Leo casually leaning against it. The second taller man who arrived this morning stood astride a short distance away. As they appeared, he raised and aimed a gun.

Side by side and puffing, Ben and Piper halted.

'Mr. Hendry,' Ben acknowledged, his body tense, his voice gravel hard.

'When you didn't contact me about the girl, I had my guys find and track you.' Hendry flicked a glance at Piper before his tight mouth and steely stare cut Ben down. 'You changed teams.'

'I prefer to be given the facts. And I always choose the *right* side of the law.'

'You're on the wrong side now.' Hendry nodded to Leo. 'Go and get it.'

Leo straightened away from the motorbike and started toward Ben.

Piper rasped out a desperate, '*No!*'

She turned to Ben, the tragedy of this impending loss after they had just found it, mirrored in the equally devastated expression on his face.

'Guess there's no use saying we didn't find it,' he said with larrikin humour.

'Shoulda got rid of you for real when we had the chance,' Leo hissed in Piper's face as he passed.

Raising his hands as Leo approached, Ben said, 'Take it easy, man. I'll get it out for you.'

He slowly shrugged off his backpack, hunkered down to the ground and unzipped the main compartment. Piper watched his every movement with horror. Ben must have felt the same anguish because he hesitated and glanced up at her before removing what they had just found. The torment reflected in his eyes clearly conveying to her that they had no choice. They were no longer in control.

After all she had been through on her own to get the hunt started, then the revealing and unlikely teaming up with Ben. Taking one step at a time. Playing one hunch at a time, using his PI resources. All for nothing now. This was one moment when Piper hoped her ancestors weren't watching. She was gutted and ashamed.

In her fog of despair, she grew aware that Ben had withdrawn the artefact, that treasured relic that they had possessed again for such a short time. What would it have been? Fifteen minutes tops?

But she might not have recovered the heirloom at all without Ben's help nor had the opportunity to even see and so briefly hold it. To have retained its tantalising possession only to have it ripped away again. This time, she was sure, forever. Armed, these guys were playing for keeps. For all involved, there was much at stake here.

As Ben handed over the artefact package to Leo and the dirtbag wrapped his greedy hands around it, Piper wanted to scream out *bastard* at the top of her lungs. He idly rolled it over, satisfied that all seemed intact as it should be.

Piper's only thoughts at that moment as possession of something so precious was transferred to a criminal, was that she had been unable to fulfil her promise to grandma and their ancestors. She had failed.

Ben and Piper, their hands now each tied behind their backs, were pushed into the back of the four wheel drive, Hendry behind the wheel, the precious package on the front passenger seat beside him.

'I'm going to owe Pete big time,' Ben muttered with unlikely humour, watching Leo discard the helmets and mount the bike.

Honestly, Piper sighed to herself, how could he joke at a disastrous time like this? If he was trying to lighten the disappointment, it didn't work.

Leo rode ahead of the car and within minutes both vehicles had returned to the airfield. Leo steered the motorbike around the side of the corrugated iron shed and their four wheel drive parked with the others in front of the building.

Ben and Piper were bundled out, marched across to the main shed and shut inside.

Chapter 10

Drained by her overwhelming emotions of despair, Piper tried to let anger overcome her sadness. But feeling utter hopelessness, tears silently slid down her face. She let them, furious with her failure. They had the relic in their hands!

Unable to see a damn thing that was happening outdoors, she guessed the plane would appear soon and the buyer would swoop on the artefact. She wished her hands weren't tied behind her back because she could block her ears, then she wouldn't have to hear the plane land and take off again, with all of her hopes and dreams inside. Never to be seen again.

Piper sat in silence for a moment on the hard concrete floor, backed up against cold walls beside Ben, freezing face and hands growing numb. Privately assessing their disastrous situation.

Ben whispered, 'Sorry for the hiccup.'

She wished. If only that's all it was. Piper pushed aside her crippling disbelief and sighed, her misery raw. 'No one's fault. Bad timing.

Thanks for all you did anyway.'

'Listen, we need to get out of here before we hear that plane.' Ben's tone was urgent. 'The moment it lands is our best window of opportunity while they're all distracted with its arrival.'

Piper was surprised by Ben's hurry to leave. She was fully aware, since Hendry had a gun, they should try to escape. Who knew what plans the thieves had in store for them after the relic transfer was done and they left? All the same, she itched to know the buyer's identity. The artwork's new owner. But far more, the relic was right here. Somewhere close.

'You don't think we should hang around for a second chance? Plan B?'

'Not looking hopeful. Four men and guns. We knew we'd have to wing it.'

Piper was annoyed that, after all their efforts so far, Ben was not more determined to try again. Okay, the odds were stacked against them and their hands were tied but so what?

'You're just giving up?'

'I know it's a stretch but can you trust me one more time.'

'Why? Give me one good reason.'

'Instinct.'

Piper scoffed. 'That old chestnut. We've been together all the time. What can you possibly know that I don't?'

Ben's voice turned soft and pleading.

'Please.'

Piper gasped in frustration. Her decision swayed between agreement because his PI skills and hunches had all delivered. So far. And fighting back.

'You have something else in mind?'

'I do.'

'Away from here? And the relic?' she challenged in disbelief.

He nodded.

'This is crazy. Whatever you have in mind, better be guaranteed like 007 or Superman-proof.'

Ben chuckled. 'Promise, but we gotta get away first.'

'How can leaving this place possibly allow us to get the relic back?' Ben just shrugged and raised his eyebrows. Piper blew out a deep frustrated breath and mumbled with resignation, 'I can't believe I'm agreeing to this.'

'So that's a *yes* and we're on the same page?'

'You better have a knife to cut these ropes because there's nothing useful in here.' She glanced around the shed.

Ben shuffled around until his back faced Piper. 'Can you fish inside my right hand side trouser pocket?'

It wasn't easy because they both still wore their backpacks and his was in the way, but she did as he asked. It was rather interesting touching Ben's backside and leg looking for the pocket and whatever was inside.

'This one?' She patted it lightly.

'Yep.'

Piper worked her fingers inside until they wrapped around something small, metal and cold, and drew it out.

'Can you transfer it into my hands?' he asked.

Piper felt around until her cold hands met his. A strangely intimate manoeuvre while they tried to untie themselves to get free. As for the escape, she had no idea what Ben was thinking but knew they would need either their motorbike or one of the enemy's vehicles to achieve it.

Piper turned around to watch what Ben was doing. He had opened up what looked like a small hunting knife and was already working the blade through his own ties. When it broke, he shook them off and quickly did the same for the rope around Piper's wrists.

With only one small window on the end wall, Ben indicated to keep low and moved across to it, carefully peering out to see where all the men were.

'Hendry's still out on the runway chasing kangaroos. Leo and Vince have their backs to us looking up, watching out for the plane. Can't see Eddie. He's probably up in the high shed communicating with the pilot but he'll be facing out over the airfield.'

'Do you pick locks too?' she asked as they moved across to the door.

Ben smiled. 'Not locked. They cut the bolt when they arrived which means they don't have keys and they're here without permission or notification. Under the radar so to speak.'

Piper groaned at the pun.

'They weren't expecting us. They're thinking on the run and making mistakes. Didn't even check our backpacks or pockets or take our phones.' His hand reached out and wrapped around the door handle. When he pushed down, it gave and the door whined ajar. 'I saw Leo wheel the motorbike around the other side. When I say *run*, head to the right around the back of this shed and wait for me.'

'Where are you going?'

'Nowhere. Trust me, I'll be right behind you.'

Anxious seconds ticked by while Ben snuck quick glances around the door. After the third time, he said 'Run!'

Piper didn't wait. Heart pounding she dashed along the shed, hugging its wall, and around the corner. As promised, Ben was only about five seconds behind.

'Had to close the door slow and quiet. Don't think they saw us.'

They edged along the back of the shed and checked around the far corner. The motorbike was parked tantalisingly close.

'Now what?' Piper asked.

'We wait until we hear that plane and all eyes are on it. Then leg it.'

The next five minutes were the longest Piper had ever known. Even if they managed to wheel the bike away into the nearby bush and a measure of cover from sight, there was no guarantee they would get away unheard once they fired the engine. Their opposition had powerful vehicles for pursuit but Ben and Piper had the advantage of overgrown bushland to snake through, making it difficult for any four wheel drive to follow. At least with any speed.

Too soon, yet not soon enough, they heard the distant drone of a small plane approaching.

'Stay here.'

Ben crept around the other side of the shed to the bike. As he pushed it past her, Piper ran alongside toward the nearby trees. She darted anxious backward glances to check if they had been seen. But all eyes of the four men were trained on the descending small plane sinking lower before it landed on the rough bush runway.

Ben caught sight of it and whistled low. 'Nice ride. Six seater low wing.'

Once among the trees and hoping the plane engine drowned out the sound, Ben legged it over the bike. It felt unprotected riding without helmets as Piper jumped on behind, grabbing him tight as he kicked the engine into life.

Hunching low, they sped through the trees, weaving around the patchy undergrowth, following narrow animal trails where they led through the bush.

With no time to waste, having to backtrack to Dunkeld to return the motorbike, neither looked back. Piper knew anyone in pursuit would need to take the same route. As the crow flies, Halls Gap was frustratingly close but, over steep and winding mountain roads, it would take all of them much longer. So neither side would have an advantage.

Somehow, Piper took comfort from that knowledge, clung on tight to Ben's waist, her pounding heart easing once they reached the main road leading south. Ben opened up the machine and they cruised on with purpose, pushing the speed limit.

Piper's emotions were mixed. They had escaped from the criminals but, having left something so precious behind, her heart broke with sadness as they drove. With Ben's skills and intuition, they had done their best and come so close.

Perhaps he had only promised a miracle to get her safely out of there. If that was his tactic, she would be grateful, even flattered, but find it damn hard to forgive. She would risk her life to get back that artwork. Impossible to talk on this thundering machine. Whatever trick Ben planned to pull out of his bike helmet better be productive.

Because it was impossible to think and feel otherwise, her thoughts centred on her disastrous loss, her future and that, really, despite everything achieved in recent weeks, nothing had changed. The prospect of facing her father with bad news, after having such high hopes and bungling grandma's final gift of opportunity. More than anything, that was the source of her angry mood.

Not soon enough, they reached Dunkeld again and returned the powerful motorbike to Pete at the garage. Ben apologised for the loss of the helmets and paid Pete out in cash. The mechanic seemed unconcerned and checked it over, satisfied there was no damage. The men warmly shook hands before Ben and Piper strode out the back.

Ben whipped off the tarpaulin cover from his hire vehicle and, as they offloaded their backpacks into the boot, he paused, reservation on his face. 'Something you should know before we leave.'

His guarded comment made Piper eye him with interest. Was this his fabulous plan? Something off-centre he needed to explain?

He was watching her with such a sense of caution she scowled with worry. He was still the same gorgeous Ben. The thick stubble on his chin did amazing things to his macho appeal. Whatever he had to say, she would probably forgive him. The knowledge made her sick and irritated. He'd been remarkably helpful and competent. If you needed to go chase criminals, he had the goods and was the man you wanted by your side.

So she prepared herself, crossed her arms and waited. 'I'm listening.'

There was no explanation. Instead, he unzipped the main compartment of his backpack. To Piper's surprise, he withdrew a cardboard cylinder similar to the one which housed her ancestral artwork. She glanced at him, a strange sense of premonition running through her mind.

'When you explained to me about your stolen relic and how it was stored, I took a punt. That morning before we left Dunkeld for the airfield two days ago, I bought this. Hoping it looked something like the original.' He withdrew a plain cardboard tube from his backpack.

Piper gaped at him with puzzled anticipation as he shrugged and continued.

'When we found the package in the cave, I opened it up, quickly checked and there wasn't a whole hell of a lot of difference, so I carefully withdrew the artefact, slipped it into this cylinder, left the original one empty, rewrapped in the leather in the plastic bag and resealed it. I figured it was better to leave the original tube and save the artwork,' his voice was remorseful.

Piper clamped a hand over her mouth. He was apologising? With each word of his explanation, shock and amazement scrolled through her body. Slowly shaking her head, she whispered, 'So this is-?'

Ben nodded.

'Shit. We need to get this out of here.'

'My thoughts exactly.'

She grabbed his arm. 'How did you even think of this?'

'Moment of inspiration,' he murmured.

On impulse she threw her arms around his neck and squeezed tight. Not the first time she had thought of doing it but the first time she put her feelings into action.

'Oh my God,' she whispered. 'Thank you, thank you, thank you. I'm stumped.'

'In a good way?' His warm breath brushed against the side of her face. His arms automatically slid around her tiny waist in response to her reaction.

She nodded against his neck because she was close to bawling her eyes out, her throat choked up with threatening tears. Her only thought was that she mustn't cry. It would make his skin wet. Besides, wasn't this a gobsmacking, burst-of-sunshine happy moment? She should be laughing. Except this revelation was so damned important, the ancestors would be looking down doing the smiling. It was perfectly fine if she cried. So she did.

Piper sobbed, her whole body shaking with the pent up sense of relief. There was no failure after all. Only success. Ben had succeeded. He had thought of this and made it happen. The guy was a genius. Her whole mob going back generations would owe him a debt and he would now become one of her people. He had earned it.

As much as she needed this moment and Ben calmly held her while she dissolved into an emotional mess, Piper knew they needed to make tracks.

So she forced herself to pull away from him and swipe at the worst of her tears. 'We need to get this thing to safety. I'm not even game to touch it.'

'Sure.'

'You don't know-'

'Yes I do,' he said softly and she felt the soft touch of his lips against her forehead. 'We're not done yet. We need to get back to your car in Halls Gap and then split up. Those guys might only be ten or fifteen minutes behind us. Depending on how long it took for the plane to land and the buyer to check it out, coming up empty. After that, I guess it was pretty much chaos.'

Now that she knew they had the real thing, Piper grew more than mildly stressed. 'We're both totally vulnerable now. They know our vehicles-'

'Don't. Let's just leave and get the hell out of here.'

They climbed into the four wheel drive and turned out onto the main street.

'Stop!' Piper said suddenly.

Ben frowned but pulled into a park. 'What? You see the men?'

She shook her head. 'No. It's Billie.' Naturally, Ben looked totally puzzled. 'She could be the solution to a problem before it even arises.'

'We don't have a problem, do we?'

'Not yet.' So Piper put forward a suggestion that even she found hard to believe she was considering.

Ben raised his eyebrows in disbelief. 'You'd part with the artwork and trust it to a stranger?

'I went to school with her.'

'Before yesterday, when did you last talk to her?'

Piper hedged. 'Not for a few years. Ben, listen. After Halls Gap when we split up, if they find either of us they'll find the artwork or kidnap or threaten the other one – or worse – until they get what they want. But what about if a third party has the artwork and takes it home?' She sent him a pleading glance. 'The guys won't be looking for her. I don't give a damn if they find me as long as they don't get their hands on that artwork again. Think about it.'

'We're wasting time we don't have,' he

groaned.

'It will only take a few minutes. She'll either help us or she won't. If not, we'll continue as planned.'

'Piper, this is damned big risk. Entrusting the relic to someone else after all we've done to get it back.'

'I know.' She shrugged. 'So what do you suggest? We stash it somewhere and come back another time?'

'Same difference.' He ran both hands through his hair and blew out a deep breath. 'Okay, let's ask this Billie but are you damn sure about her?'

Piper was wavering herself but she nodded anyway. Not having an issue with Billie's trust but her own spur-of-the-moment crazy idea. So crazy, it *had* to work. This was too vital not to.

She scrambled from the vehicle and called out to Billie across the street. Piper was amused at her friend's long-suffering glance when she recognised her. She dashed toward her and confronted her on the pavement.

'Do you have five minutes?' Billie nodded. 'When are you heading to the Wimmera?'

'Today probably.'

'Listen, I need a favour. We need your help.' Billie peered over Piper's shoulder. 'My friend, Ben and I, need something delivered to, say, the Coach Roadhouse on the highway? Are you heading in that direction?'

Billie hesitated. 'I could.'

'Great.' Piper rubbed her hands together. 'We have to go pick up my car from Halls Gap so if we give you something, could you meet us at the roadhouse in about an hour?'

'Why can't you take it yourself?'

Truth time. 'We have an old family heirloom that was stolen from my mob years ago. We just found it and the thieves are trying to get it back. They'll recognise us but not you.'

Noticing Billie's justifiable hesitation and fearful she might change her mind, Piper launched into a rushed babbled explanation of the recent days' events.

A deep emptiness landed in the pit of her stomach when she finished and Billie remained silent for far too long. Piper could see the conflict on Billie's face as she processed the significance of what she had just been asked. Well, at least they tried. After bailing up Billie on the street and with such a thin account, was she even fair to ask such an obligation of a friend she grew up with but hadn't seen for years?

'It's okay. I get it.' Piper tried to be polite but was unable to keep disappointment from her voice.

Billie suddenly held up a hand. 'Whoa! You telling me those greedy bastards did this to your own family? Something so precious? How low is that?'

Piper roused with optimism at Billie's

spluttered reaction. It was like another deeper part of her friend had suddenly kicked into life.

'Honestly,' Billie's outrage increased, 'some people have no concept of humanity and decency. Screw people over, take advantage, for entirely selfish reasons.'

At Billie's indignant outburst, Piper thought her friend's fiercely raw response seemed personal. Maybe she wasn't only mad on Piper's behalf but had experienced something equally deceitful.

Billie planted her hands on her hips, took a deep breath and stared at Piper, brown eyes flashing. 'I know exactly how you feel. Being wrongly blamed with some twisted scheming to make you feel guilty without reason when it's someone else's fault.'

Piper's heart went out to Billie for whatever nasty experience she had suffered, too. 'Does this mean you'll help us?'

'Absolutely,' Billie replied with conviction.

'Oh my God, we're so grateful.' She leant forward to give her friend an instinctive hug. 'Follow me.'

Piper grabbed Billie by the arm and led her across to the vehicle. At their approach, Ben leapt out, popped the boot and was rummaging in his backpack as the women reached him. Piper made quick introductions all round. Ben nodded to Billie as he handed over the artefact.

'Guard it with your life.' Piper pleaded. 'It's

priceless.'

'No pressure,' Billie said wryly.

They exchanged phone numbers, arranged to meet up soon at the Coach Roadhouse and separated.

As Billie walked away with the cylinder in the large carryall slung over her shoulder, while Piper and Ben climbed back into their vehicle, she whispered, 'What have we done?'

'Kept it safe.'

Ben laid a reassuring hand on her knee, backed out and sped off toward the intersection on the outskirts of town where they turned to head north and Halls Gap. They decided this direct route was faster, if not safer. It had been an hour from the airfield into Dunkeld on the motor bike, they spent time at the garage and with Billie which took another ten minutes. Which meant valuable time had ticked away and the men, assuming they would be followed, would be close behind.

Ben sped back through the mountains to reclaim Piper's vehicle. Every kilometre that passed, they both anxiously checked their mirrors.

Reaching Halls Gap, apparently unnoticed, they decided to split up, driving independently back to the roadhouse, each taking a different route. Ben set up Piper's phone so they could track each other. They agreed the first one to arrive at the Coach would send a coded text to the other to let them know they had arrived safely and were waiting.

'What happens if one of us is caught?' Piper wondered out loud, sensing they needed to cover the worst possible outcome.

Ben frowned. 'If we have time, call and maybe just leave the phone on to hear any conversation and voices. Let the other know what's happening and the potential situation.'

On a phone map, Piper showed Ben two possible routes back to the highway and then the roadhouse, both only taking about thirty minutes so they should arrive reasonably close together.

Piper suggested, 'I'll take the Mount Drummond Road back to the highway. Has a few more twists and turns. You take this one,' she pointed on the map. 'The Mount Dryden Road. It's a more direct route. Runs north before turning to go through Roses Gap and meets up with the highway further on.'

As Piper turned to climb into her car, Ben reached out for her hand, tugged her close and brushed his mouth across hers in a whisper-soft kiss. 'Take care,' he murmured. 'See you soon.'

Piper grew still, Ben's casual unexpected gesture catching her by surprise. Speechless with delight, she nodded and finally managed an awkward, 'Yeah, right.'

She sank into her car with a stupid grin on her face. Four days. She had only known this guy four days. Disliked him on sight and look how that turned out. Maybe living with tension heightened emotions. Piper's concern now was that they might fade.

Not a woman to flirt for a man's attention, she was always intrigued by one who made the first move. Wondering what it was about her that caught his interest. Gave her a breather to check him out up close. Quietly observe him while he bought her a drink or chatted. Or, in Ben's case, bailed her up in a bush carpark. The memory filled her with a glow of warmth and kick of amusement.

So her thoughts were full and cheerful as she drove away, Ben's silver four wheel drive once more in her rear mirrors until they parted ways a few kilometres out of Halls Gap. He flashed his lights behind her when she turned onto the side road, heading across country toward the highway and roadhouse while he continued on.

Despite feeling so light hearted, Piper knew a sense of caution. For everything Ben had achieved for her mission and her attraction now compared to the first day they met. In half an hour, they would be reunited with the artefact and each other. But then what? Would they keep in touch? Would she ever see him again? They had started out as enemies but joining forces on this quest had brought them closer. Was there a spark for that reason alone, or more? Maybe she would find out at the roadhouse.

Piper had never had a serious boyfriend or partner, always restless, moving on. Never allowing herself the experience of a man in her life for longer than weeks or months. Deliberately holding back from forming a committed relationship.

Would retrieving the tribal artwork and putting it back into her father's rightful hands, finally give her the release she subconsciously craved from the dreadful emotional heaviness that had weighed her down all these years?

Piper kept checking her mirrors but all seemed quiet. No trailing vehicle behind. So when she turned onto the highway, she knew Ben would only be about five to ten minutes and a few kilometres behind.

The prospect lifted her heart. An honest dependable man had entered her life. The relic was safe with Billie. The future looked promising and she couldn't wait to see what it brought.

A few kilometres away, Ben's gaze flicked into his rear view mirror to see a distant vehicle gaining on him and groaned. 'Shit. Company.'

The familiar BMW had snuck up on him fast since the last corner. With one hand on the wheel, he fumbled, trying to grab his phone, but it was too late. His thoughts instantly flashed to Piper. She and the artwork were safe.

Chapter 11

As Piper pulled into the Coach Roadhouse, she noticed with relief Billie's SUV was already in the carpark. With a light step, she slung her backpack over one shoulder and strode inside. Scanning the restaurant, Piper acknowledged Billie's wave from a table by the window.

'Hi Holly,' she greeted the waitress as she passed the counter.

'Piper. You heading away again?'

She gestured toward Billie. 'Catching up with a friend first.'

'Nice.'

A shadow of longing more than envy crossed Holly's face. Piper's heart went out to her, wondering if the waitress had many friends of her own. Having moved here five years ago following her mother's disappearance in the area, maybe other family and friends lived elsewhere.

Piper slid into a seat opposite Billie. 'Such a relief to be here now the getaway is safely done. We can't thank you enough for doing this.'

'It was actually a bit exciting. And a

privilege to be trusted with such an historic treasure.' Billie glanced beyond Piper toward the door. 'Ben not with you?'

'We took separate roads. Just a precaution. He'll be here any moment.'

'Should I hand over the relic to you now?'

'You know what? I didn't even have the courage to touch it when Ben revealed he had managed to swap it over into a fake tube. After years of being lost, it suddenly made our discovery real. Scary, realising I possessed such an important artefact again. I'm half expecting to lose it again.'

'You didn't lose it in the first place though, did you?' Billie pointed out.

Heartened by her correction, Piper took a deep anxious breath. 'Okay, I'll take a quick peek now. Just to reassure myself.'

Billie handed over the long roll of artwork. Piper accepted it like delicate glass that might break at any moment. She grabbed a table napkin, using it as protection from her hands as she slowly withdrew it from the cylinder a few centimetres. Reassured she was looking at the genuine article for the first time in five years since it was stolen, Piper stared at the familiar rough edges and brittle state of the bark before gently sliding the painted work back inside.

'It's as colourful and amazing as I remember.'

'Can't believe it has survived so long.'

'I can assure you, being so meaningful to my people, it was cherished. And spoken of with awe and respect,' Piper said proudly.

'And you've returned it to its rightful place,' Billie quietly observed.

'With your help. We've already interrupted your day. I don't want to hold you up if you need to be somewhere else but can I buy you a celebratory coffee while we wait for Ben?'

'Sure. Thanks.'

'Great. I'm starving. With early action this morning at the airfield, we missed breakfast.'

Heading for the counter, Piper noted Billie's less troubled mood since meeting her in Dunkeld the first time a few days ago. The healing effect of a stopover in the mountains maybe?

As Holly took her order and, since the restaurant appeared temporarily quieter before the lunchtime rush, Piper suggested, 'I know you're working but if you can spare a few minutes while we're here, come over and join us?'

Holly's smile lit up her face. After a quick glance behind her, she said, 'Okay, thanks,' and nodded toward a young woman serving nearby. 'Sophie can cover for me and Gracie's always around for backup. I'll bring over your order.'

Piper didn't know why she felt compelled to reach out to Holly. Something intangible stirred her empathy. The air of a lonesome soul

160

perhaps. Not dissimilar to her own life situation.

As Piper strolled back to their table, she wondered if finding the artefact would change her personal circumstances in any way. If at all. Whether she would feel more at ease returning home to visit. Receive a warmer welcome from some of her mob when she did. Until she experienced their reactions to the relic's return, which she imagined would be positive, even forgiving, there was no way to predict her reception.

She had grown so comfortable as a wanderer. Independent to pursue her painting career and freely travel this beautiful country.

Another factor was Ben. She didn't know too much about him. Yet. Just that his parents had died and he was an only child. Did he have any close mates and friends? She mentally crossed her fingers and rather hoped she had the chance to see him again. Learn more about the man who had gallantly taken her side and more than captured her attention.

Getting to know Ben, a man worth much more than a second look, had drawn out considerations in her mind. Like, what was potentially missing in her life. A compatible partner. Ben had so easily slipped in under her emotional radar. Demonstrated by her reaction to his kiss before they left Halls Gap. It had hit the spot. A bloke didn't kiss a girl like that without it meaning something.

'I invited Holly to join us,' Piper said to Billie as she sat down again, checking the time. 'Ben will be hungry when he arrives.' She frowned. 'Should be almost here.'

Despite Billie's company, waiting for him was a kind of gnawing expectation. Thankfully, Holly appeared with their drinks and snacks. A timely distraction.

'Sophie and Gracie are relieving me,' she said, as she took a seat beside Piper. She glanced between the other women. 'Have you been friends long?'

'Since school,' Piper said. 'Incredibly we ran into each other by chance in Dunkeld.'

Holly brightened with interest. 'What were you doing down there?'

Not that Piper didn't trust Holly but she was emotionally bushed. Right now, she lacked the energy to elaborate. There would be another time for details. So she merely said, 'Camping for a few days before I head back to the coast.' A generalisation but nonetheless true.

'And, as coincidence would have it, I was on my way up to Reedy Lake,' Billie offered. 'We met again today as we were both leaving. Piper suggested we meet here before parting ways again.'

'The lake's idyllic in winter,' Holly told Billie. 'Fogs on the surface. Pelicans, black swans and ducks galore.'

'Yes, I remember. I haven't been back in

while,' Billie admitted.

'It's important to keep in touch with family,' Holly said with more than a hint of nostalgia.

Piper knew her comment wasn't a criticism but probably came from a deep empty place of unresolved maternal loss in her heart that may never be filled.

When a huge B-Double rig pulled in off the highway to the roadhouse transport parking area, Holly's attention sparked. The tall muscled driver climbed down, pushed a well-worn Akubra onto his head and walked around his truck, checking all was in order. Satisfied, his easy rolling gait brought him across to the restaurant.

Piper watched Holly abruptly stand, her cheeks flushed. 'I guess I should get back. Lunch customers will be here soon.'

'Sure. Take care.'

Billie leaned forward. 'Interesting?'

'She was so embarrassed,' Piper said. 'I have my back to them so tell me what's happening.'

'She's hovering behind the counter. Pretending to be busy. Sophie is serving him.'

'How can a twenty-something be so shy?'

Billie grew thoughtful. 'That truckie *means* something to her.' She sounded almost resentful.

'He's certainly a knockout.'

Piper watched Billie's relaxed mood darken. Was her lake break a *heartbreak*? If so, romance had a lot to answer for. Thinking of eye-catching men, she flicked a glance at her phone clock. She suddenly realised that, since chatting with the girls, Ben was now running late!

'Anything wrong?' Billie asked.

Piper frowned. 'Ben should be here by now.'

'Call him.'

Piper was swamped by a bad feeling. She pressed his number but it rang out. 'No answer.'

Filled with the worst kind of dread, Piper opened the tracking app. 'He's still on the Roses Gap Road. Hasn't even reached the highway yet. And he's not moving.'

'So, he stopped for a moment.'

Piper shook her head. 'Has no reason. We both intended to drive straight here.'

'Could be a breakdown?'

'He would have called to let me know.' Piper swallowed over her dry throat. 'By some cruel stroke of fate, I bet they've found him.'

'The thieves? Don't jump to conclusions. There's probably a perfectly ordinary explanation.'

'You don't know them. They're armed. Somehow they've caught up with Ben before he's even had time to grab his phone. I can't take them on alone. I need help. Be sensible about this and plan.'

'How many of them?'

'At least two, possibly all four from the airfield, or even more if the guy in the plane tagged along. I feel sick,' Piper moaned as she made a call. 'Dad?'

'So good to hear from you at last.'

On hearing his voice, Piper knew she should have called from Dunkeld or Halls Gap to let him know her whereabouts. He would be concerned. He could have met them here. So Piper quickly updated her father and explained. First about the rescued artefact and that it was safe. In Jimmy's silence, clearly overcome, Piper went on to explain that Ben was missing. She spared a reflective moment for Holly. Is this heart-stopping shock how it felt when someone you loved disappeared?

Over her anxiety, Jimmy was saying, 'I can be out there in ten minutes. I'll have backup.'

She hung up. With her mind in a spin, Piper said, 'Should I call the police?'

'Can you?'

Piper sighed. 'I know one of the local cops, Ewan Holt. Not sure it warrants his attention though. This is a personal matter gone wrong.'

'You don't know that for sure yet.'

'Until we get out there and identify the problem, there's probably not a lot the police can do anyway.' She indicated her phone. 'I know exactly where he is. He could be injured. Or worse.'

On that thought, Piper almost cracked. Ben had been drawn into her family drama. Ultimately his choice but she felt responsible now for his safety.

'Billie, you're probably keen to head to the lake.'

'No rush. I'll wait until your father arrives.'

'Thanks.' Piper rose and carefully carried the artefact cylinder to the counter, catching caught Holly's attention. 'Do you have a bulletproof safe?'

'Yes.'

'Do you think Sid and Gracie would mind if I locked something in it for a while?'

'Of course not. Follow me.'

Holly beckoned her around the end of the counter and led the way along a back passage into an office. The door was ajar but she only briefly knocked and barged in. Gracie Townsend, with her wild crown of long grey hair and red glasses, looked up from her desk computer.

'Piper needs to put something in Bertie.'

The safe had a name?

Gracie seemed neither alarmed nor unconcerned, accepting Holly's request. 'Sure.'

The older woman rose and tapped in the combination on a keypad beside the inbuilt wall safe. Then stood aside as Piper slid the cylinder inside.

'If no one returns for this,' Piper said, 'can you make sure it's delivered to the Elders of my local people?'

Gracie raised her eyebrows, her mouth quirked in amusement. 'Sure, sweetie, but where are you going and why aren't you coming back?'

Feeling the weight of Ben's probable capture, Piper wasn't sure she appreciated Gracie's light-hearted reaction. 'Instinct. And a precaution.'

While Ben's hunch about the airfield and hers about the hiding place of the artefact both proved right, this time Piper hoped she would be wrong.

At least Gracie had the courtesy to grasp Piper's serious response. 'Trouble? Can we help?'

'Not at the moment. Thanks for asking.' After a pause, she blurted out, 'Actually, my friend's missing.'

When Gracie and Holly shared an understanding glance, Piper could have bit her tongue. She didn't think... Holly's mother...

'I'm sure he's fine but I need to check. Could be a tricky situation.' *Keep fooling yourself. It will help push your fears aside.*

Distracted by the upheaval happening in her head, Piper thanked Gracie and strode back into the restaurant. For no reason, her gaze skimmed the room. A few families and other travellers. The truck driver sat alone at a window table. Billie stood waiting for her at theirs.

'I need fresh air,' Piper said. 'I'm going outside to wait for Dad. Are you leaving for the lake now?'

Billie chuckled. 'As if. When you go to find

Ben, I'm coming too.'

'Oh, you can't-'

'Yes I can. Don't argue. I do taekwondo. I kick butt. Literally. I'll be handy to have around.'

A speechless Piper marvelled at the strong change in Billie's approach. Where did the fierce warrior woman suddenly come from?

They waited outside together. Piper kept impatiently glancing at the time on her phone, desperate for a message from Ben. Checking every minute achieved nothing except making her doubly anxious. But every idle moment potentially placed Ben deeper in danger.

Finally, twelve minutes later - she knew exactly how long, because she had watched every single one of them drag by - help arrived. And they were all in Gilbert's powerful vehicle. Perfect if they needed a quick getaway car. Nothing would catch them in that machine. Piper grinned through her unease over Ben as Gilbert's large frame unravelled and climbed out from the driver's seat, grinning broadly.

'I was at the farm visiting your parents to see if they had any news of you when you phoned.'

Her father soon appeared alongside. Overwhelmed with affection and relief at the sight of the man who had always been her rock and champion, she burst into tears as they hugged. Words vanished.

When she recovered herself and swiped her

wet cheeks, it was to see Coen, of all people, hovering in the background. Deliberately invited? Ready to right a wrong? And her brother?

'Yarran! Dad,' she turned to him in appeal, 'should the boys come along? This will be risky and could turn nasty.'

'We'll watch out for them,' he assured his daughter. 'Your mother's done the phone tree thing and alerted the mob.'

Word had been dispersed among their people? At this point, Piper didn't understand how contacting everyone could help. They would worry for nothing. And her fears could be a false alarm, or easily explained.

Nonetheless, stunned by the degree of support, she said, 'Thank you guys but we need to split.' She introduced Billie all around and shook her head. 'Gil, they'll hear you coming in that car but we may need the horsepower. The thieves know my vehicle so Billie and I will take her SUV.' She turned to her friend for confirmation and Billie nodded. 'I'll navigate and we'll take the lead. Gil? You, Dad and Coen stay a distance behind. Just keep us in sight okay? Yarry, want to ride with us?'

Her young vulnerable brother brightened and stepped forward.

'We head south to the Roses Gap Road. When we reach the target spot, slow to a crawl or they'll hear us coming. We'll probably need to park further back and go in on foot.'

'Gotcha, girlie.' Gil gave a thumbs up and everyone strode for their wheels.

Chapter 12

Piper took up the passenger seat beside Billie, keeping an eye on her phone tracker and giving directions. Within minutes they had turned off the highway, practically on top of Ben's signal.

'We should stop,' Piper urged Billie. 'He's off to the left.'

She pulled over. In the rear mirrors, Piper noticed Gilbert do the same behind them. Everyone stayed in their vehicles. The most horrible thoughts and worst possible outcomes raced through Piper's mind. They might find Ben's discarded phone and nothing else. He could be kidnapped. Not even here. Nowhere to be found. A crippling prospect.

Because she couldn't entertain the idea that she wouldn't see Ben soon, Piper forced her outlook to be positive.

Only then did the urgency of the situation kick into play. Ben needed to be rescued and a plan put in place to do it. In low tones, as though she might be overheard, Piper began processing ideas.

'We need to go see what's happening.

Someone small with less chance of being seen. Experienced in the bush and best chance of being silent.'

'I can go, sis,' Yarran offered quietly from the back seat.

Piper had almost forgotten he was there. Blown away by his courage, she knew he could have no idea how risky such surveillance would be. She turned to her brother, seeing him for the first time as a young man emerging from the vulnerable boy. Encouraged by the change.

'That's brave of you, Yarry. Thanks for offering but I'll recognise the guys so it's probably best I do this quick recon first. We'll need your help soon enough. Okay?'

He nodded, accepting her decision. Piper phoned Gilbert and explained her recon plan.

'Feel better if I came along too, girlie,' he muttered.

'I'll need your brawn to come get me if I'm nabbed.' She heard him grunt in disapproval. 'I'll take my phone on silent. See if I can't get some photos.'

'No crazy moves, eh?'

'If I'm not back in five minutes, come find me. Wish me luck,' Piper said as she climbed from Billie's car, not fully closing the door in case the sound travelled.

She paused before moving off, standing still, absorbing the feel of her surroundings. Listening. Then, careful where she placed her feet, believing she heard distant sounds and voices, she headed in that direction further along.

Somehow, knowing it was Ben in need of rescue lent Piper strength to do this. Forget herself. Focus on the logistics of who and how many men, where they were in relation to each other. And most importantly, where Ben was and in what physical condition. Whether it looked like they had hurt or tied him. If he was even there. *Don't*, she told herself.

Keeping low and creeping closer, stepping carefully, Piper halted the moment she caught sight of people through the scrub.

Five men. Piper could have cried and choked back a gasp of relief. Ben. And the other four from the airfield. No new faces. The mystery buyer nowhere to be seen.

Ben sat on the ground backed up against a gnarled eucalypt, his hands tied behind him. Facing in her direction. Looking up at Hendry and Leo, who appeared to be questioning him, standing over Ben with their backs to Piper. There was an opportunity here.

Casting a quick glance to Vince and Eddie off to one side leaning against the BMW pulled in behind Ben's four wheel drive, Piper moved around behind the slender trunk of a young gum. Looking twice to make sure she was hidden enough before moving, Piper stood up to reveal herself. Ben's gaze clearly caught her movement and snapped in her direction.

She dropped down again, her heart racing with adrenalin and lifting with hope. He had seen her and would know help was here.

After zooming in to click some identifying shots of the men on her phone camera, Piper didn't waste another moment. She sneaked back to Billie's car.

On speaker phone, so all occupants of both vehicles could hear and contribute to the conversation, Piper's first words were, 'Ben's there. Seems okay.'

Then she relayed what she saw and sent her photos to Gilbert and Jimmy's mobiles.

'Ben's vehicle and the black BMW are parked just in off the road.' She outlined where each man was located and gave detailed descriptions of each one to help in identification of each person's mark. 'I wish Ben was here. He would know what to do. Maybe half of us should attack from one side, the other half from the opposite side to divide their attention. What do you think?'

'Makes sense,' she heard her father say.

'Gilbert's muscle and Billie's skill will be our best weapons. She does martial arts,' Piper explained. 'Coen and Yarran, you're strapping teenagers but not a lot of strength yet so you take on short and stubby Eddie together.'

'Maybe aim for low in the stomach,' Billie suggested.

Piper grinned. Good to know some strategy. 'Dad, can you take Vince and, Billie, you deal with Leo? He's bigger than his mate so he would probably suit your extra moves.'

'What about you?' Billie grinned, as if she didn't know.

'I'll circle around the other side to Ben. Once he's free, it will be more manpower on our side. The men's positions might change before we get there. As soon as we reach the edge of the bush and the cover of undergrowth before the small clearing, find your target and move in as close as you can without being seen.'

Between them all in the cars, suggestions flying back and forth, they worked out a strategy. Each person would work their way around close to their designated man.

'My main concern is that Hendry has a gun,' Piper said. 'I didn't see it but I imagine he'll keep it handy.'

'I'll take him on,' Gilbert volunteered.

Piper had no doubt he would and was relying on his offer. She just hoped Hendry didn't produce the gun and point it at him while he did. Some of Piper's cousins were best ignored but Gilbert Thorne was a keeper.

She didn't want any of their team to be badly hurt but admitted that there were bound to be some injuries. She only hoped they were minor. It was a probable given that, if one or more of them found themselves in serious trouble, Gilbert would be watching out for them and spring to their help.

Finally they decided that, at a given signal, they would race in, yelling, heading directly for their designated target. The idea was to collide into them with enough force that the surprise attack would unbalance or knock them over. At least, that was the plan. Giving the Thorne mob a chance of better odds at making their opposition less effective. If only temporarily. After that, it was up to each of them to keep their man subdued as best as possible.

Both Jimmy and Gilbert seemed calm and unperturbed as they all quietly left the two vehicles, speaking in whispers. They had no weapons. Just their wits.

After they split up and went in two separate directions, the groups stole slowly through the undergrowth to within sight of their objectives. Piper wondered if everyone's hearts were pounding as strongly as her own.

Crouching, they all took a moment to visually hone in on their individual target, waiting for Gilbert to stand up, raise his arm and drop it. The signal to strike.

If Piper hadn't been so nervous, she might have laughed at the thought. A bunch of amateurs taking on dangerous criminals. But they had anger and determination driving the blood in their veins.

Then Gilbert stood up, dropped his arm and

it was on.

The noise shattered the quiet of the small clearing in the bush as five people dashed in from both sides. As she crouched low, finding her way around to Ben, Piper darted a quick glance to see what was happening.

Billie's high kicks had already made easy work of combating Leo and she was wrestling him to the ground. Her father was pummelling and fending off Vince, neither winning nor losing. An even match so she was tempted to go and help, improve his odds. The boys rammed into Eddie, now flat on his back on the ground, Coen and Yarran holding him down.

Piper finally reached Ben and began to untie him. Without a word before she had finished, he nodded in front of him. Gilbert and Hendry stood apart, Hendry with his back to them pointing a gun at her cousin.

Piper sucked in a gasp. *No!* Gilbert was about to be a father.

With her only thought for his safety, she lunged forward to kick Hendry hard from behind, planting one foot on his backside. He unbalanced and pitched forward. The gun spilled from Hendry's hand and Gilbert jammed his foot on it. Kicking it aside, he stood towering over Hendry, waiting for the man to rise.

'Great work,' Ben grinned and winked as Piper turned back to fully untie him.

They rose together and hugged. He

squeezed her tight and pressed his warm lips to her mouth.

As they pulled apart, he suddenly glanced over her shoulder and stiffened. Ben released Piper and ran across to help Jimmy, struggling to overpower Vince. Eventually, with the extra manpower, he was restrained. Everyone else seemed to either have their target at bay or reasonably managed and under control.

Rumpled and breathing heavily, the thieves, now outnumbered and contained, glared at their invaders.

'Why are you still chasing us?' Ben demanded, returning to stand beside Piper. 'We escaped but you have the artwork.' He placed an arm around her shoulders, drawing her closer.

'No, we don't,' Hendry growled.

Since Ben's strategy appeared to be casting doubt into the minds of the thieves, Piper played along. This could be fun.

Straight faced and strengthened by the wonderful feeling of Ben's body close to hers, she innocently asked, 'Why not?'

'It wasn't in the bloody cylinder.'

'Really?' Piper loved how calm and convincing Ben sounded when he was about to lie. 'Man, we thought the relic was in the damn package as well. It was hard to hand it over.'

If Piper didn't know otherwise, she would have believed him herself.

'Maybe the artwork was never in the cave at

all,' Ben loaded up more doubt.

Now Hendry and Vince shot dark looks across at Leo. 'Taylor?' Hendry roared.

'I swear I hid it in the cave when the cops were after me before I was arrested. I've been in gaol ever since,' Leo spluttered.

'You didn't swap it before we arrived?' Hendry challenged.

'No. Vince was with me all the time.' He turned to his mate. 'Tell 'em Vinnie.'

'Minetti?' Hendry demanded.

'Yeah, yeah. Leo didn't go nowhere once we got to the airfield.'

'Then where the hell is it?' Hendry slowly rolled his gaze around everyone in the gathering.

'Don't look at my family,' Piper said, afraid one of them might be singled out for attention. 'We all came to help find Ben.'

Hendry rounded on Ben. 'I told you to find the girl, not take her side. If you'd done what you were supposed to and we got her out of the way, none of this would have happened.'

'There are no sides here, Hendry,' Ben said easily. 'We both know hiring me was a ploy. When I did my job and found her, she told me the true story about how the artwork came to be lost. Seems there's little truth to your side of the story at all. Everyone here,' his gaze flashed around the supporting Thorne family members, Billie and the thieves, 'knows that relic was stolen from Piper's family. That's where it really belongs.'

'Maybe we've all been betrayed,' Piper added firmly, absolutely certain she would never reveal the truth of who really betrayed who. Happy to sow even more seeds of doubt. This rescue mission had been about righting a wrong.

Since the gathering seemed to be at a standoff, she wondered what would happen next and grew concerned. The answer emerged slowly around them from the bush.

One by one, silently stepping forward into the open, members of her mob, olive skinned and dark skinned, men and women, made their appearance until they completely ringed the crowd. Their mere presence alone threatening.

Piper's gaze flew to her father. Jimmy just grinned and gave her a thumbs up. He organised this! Her heart almost burst with joy and relief.

'Back off, brother,' the leader said loud and clear to Hendry. 'Leave our people alone. This hunt is over.'

Since her mother had done the ring-around, they would all know that the artwork was safe. Word had also clearly travelled among everyone, probably broadcast by Jimmy, that her ally Ben was in trouble. Without hesitation, they had come to support the search for him in the simplest way by outnumbering the thieves with people power.

Surrounded, there was no escape for the defeated guilty group.

As Piper gazed over to see a silent Hendry's reaction, he was clearly stunned. Speechless, helpless. The furious expression on his face told her he already knew his mission and all its manipulations had failed. Ben had wised up and changed sides.

The Thorne mob had won. But she wasn't yet convinced Hendry, although bested for now, was prepared to give up. He had not said or done anything to prove he would back off from pursuit of the artwork or Piper. She would bet anything he still had them both in his sights. And she didn't like the feeling.

So amidst a feeling of deep happiness, that all had turned out right for her family, and its precious treasured legacy was recovered and safe, Piper still worried both for her own and Ben's welfare, keeping in mind any potential future actions by Hendry. In her heart, she believed he would never give up.

Over her troubled thoughts and the present deadlock between her mob and the criminals, she caught a flash of something back in the bush.

With stealth and speed from behind her mob, Ewan Holt led a squad of fellow police officers, immediately and swiftly moving in. Piper realised then that her people were the brave front line of this more purposeful second surprise contingent that followed.

Teams of blue uniforms and plain clothes swarmed in on each of the thieves. Rights were read out, handcuffs clipped on. Objections loudly raised, especially by Hendry. Leo and Vince argued and swore at each other. Eddie just glowered in shock.

'Piper, Ben and Jimmy, can you stick around?' Ewan Holt said hastily amid the action. 'I need a word with you all.'

They nodded, joining their family members and Billie to one side, watching the proceedings with awe and surprise.

Finally Piper had a moment to hug and acknowledge her father. As always, he stood patiently waiting. As she approached him, Piper broke down. With a watery smile, she slid into Jimmy's open welcoming arms, sinking into their comfort and security.

Perhaps it was the anticlimax after all that had happened to her in recent weeks. Being constantly on the go and on the run. Moving one step forward at a time.

More than that, it was Jimmy's organisation of wider backup, gathering members of their mob together. All quietly standing by in the bush, watching the confrontation and action, ready to step in and help if it was needed. Piper thought to herself they had been an inexperienced gang, taking on the criminals, thinking they were doing it alone. When in fact, had they only known it, they were being watched at all times and under protection.

When she had gathered herself together again, Piper beckoned to Ben and he stepped forward.

'Dad, this is Ben Powell. The private investigator who was hired by Hendry to find me and report back to him. Not sure what Hendry planned to do with me but thank goodness I never found out. Ben and I had a *conversation* in the bush when we met.'

'In the pouring rain,' Ben chimed in, grinning.

When Piper matched his adoring gaze, something wonderful and powerful kicked into life. Despite the cold, her whole body reacted and filled with warmth. A deep sense of caring and affection rose up and surged through her heart.

Somehow she managed to go on. 'Turned out we were actually on the same side, although we didn't quite believe it at the time. Without Ben, I would never have recovered the artwork alone.'

'I appreciate everything you have done to help my daughter.'

'You're welcome, Sir.' Ben reached out to Jimmy and they shook hands.

The gesture both lent Piper strength and caused her concern. Ben mattered to her now. More than she dared admit. Their lives were complicated, travelling on different paths. Yet, despite potential difficulties, she couldn't bear the thought of never seeing Ben again.

She pushed the unwanted thoughts from her mind. Now was not the time.

Transferring her attention back to their bush surroundings and the reason for being here, Piper slid her gaze around everyone.

'You guys were all amazing. Is everyone okay?'

Some abrasions and likely future bruises were proudly presented almost as a badge of honour for their efforts. The element of surprise had won the day.

'And Billie, you sure held your own. That high kicking and turning around thing you did?'

Her friend grinned. 'Glad to be of service.' She hesitated. 'You've helped me, Piper. I should be thanking you.'

'Listen Billie, we have Ben and Gilbert's vehicles to take everyone home. If you want to head off, you go.' Piper watched a tussle of uncertainty in her friend's expression. 'Go,' she urged. 'All's well.'

'You sure?'

'Absolutely.'

They hugged, Billie said her goodbyes, with words of thanks echoing through the bush from everyone and the promise of honorary membership of the Thorne mob as a result. As her friend walked away, Piper mentally wished her peace and sent up a plea to her ancestors to help make that happen.

Excited chatter rolled around them from each family member about the nervous exhilaration of barging into the clearing to try and overpower the thieves. Coen and Yarran teased and elbowed each other, having teamed up in support of their mob. Piper quietly looked on and smiled, convinced Jimmy had used his authority as an Elder to urge their cooperation.

Having experienced the reward of selfless help for a good cause, maybe now Coen and Yarran would grow and mature in a better understanding of the cooperation and responsibility necessary being part of not only their own, but also a wider family. Yet Piper couldn't stop a gnawing disappointment that Coen should somehow be brought to account for the deliberate and thoughtless passing on of information that led to the artwork's disappearance in the first place. Maybe it was enough that he had at least grudgingly given them the lead to narrow down the area where it may have been hidden.

Suddenly Jimmy nodded toward Piper and nudged Gilbert. 'Tell her the news.'

Gilbert beamed, saying nothing. Always a man of few words. Piper stared curiously at him for a moment before her brain clicked. 'Oh, Leyla! She's had the baby?'

Gilbert nodded, his face glowing. 'Boy.'

Piper engulfed the bottom two thirds of him in a hug. He was too big to grab in one armful, at least for a tiny person like herself. 'Congratulations. Mum and baby fine?' Gilbert nodded. 'Name?'

'Gillie Junior.'

'A great honour. Your little man will have your example to look up to. I'll bet he's perfect. I can't wait to meet him.'

As Piper and her immediate family debriefed among themselves, the Thorne mob who had so willingly appeared in support began to slowly gather around. She was overwhelmed and humbled when they approached with hugs, hands warmly extended, murmured greetings, good wishes and deep thanks for putting herself at risk in retrieving the artwork. Plus more eager questions about how it had all happened.

'We'll have a handover ceremony soon in celebration,' Jimmy said. 'Our place and everyone's invited. Spread the word. You'll hear all about it then,' he said proudly.

A future oral story to be passed down through the coming generations. This seemed to satisfy them and they all gradually dispersed to return home.

As the clearing thinned and the thieves were each individually escorted away by pairs of policemen, Ewan Holt strode forward.

'Ben, I need you to drop into the station tomorrow for a statement about being detained against your will and to give evidence in other possible convictions for the gang.

'Piper and Jimmy. I'll need you to come in for a detailed statement of what went down five years ago when the artwork was stolen.' They both nodded. 'It will add to our case against these guys. Especially Hendry. He's been dealing in the illegal theft and acquisition of indigenous artworks for years. Eddie Shaw and Vince Minetti will be arrested as accomplices.

'Looting of antiquities has a long history. The creation of beauty inspires a desire to steal and possess it.' Ewan shrugged. 'The artwork pieces usually weigh little and can be worth millions. So criminals continue to take the risk.

'Leo Taylor will have other charges to answer as well since he actually stole the artwork. Plus he's breached his parole conditions by missing a supervision appointment. Might end up back in gaol.'

Piper and her father listened in amazement, realising Coen would just have been an innocent manipulated pawn in the criminals' operations. Hopefully the lad had learnt his lesson and would take only positives away with him from the experience into the future.

Once all police vehicles had driven away, Jimmy said tactfully, 'Piper, Ben could probably drive you back to the roadhouse for your car and that precious artwork. The lads and I will all head back with Gilbert.'

Piper felt an arm slip around her waist. 'Happy to oblige,' Ben drawled.

'Your mother's expecting you,' Jimmy added. 'Laying on a feast.'

'Sure, Dad.' With raised eyebrows, she glanced up at Ben. 'We'll see you at home?' He nodded.

Piper couldn't help thinking *this would be a first. Piper bringing home a man.* Didn't mean anything but the invitation was a gesture to a stranger her family didn't know, and she appreciated it. Without Ben, none of their success would have been possible. If she was honest, alone she would probably have failed.

Still processing the happenings of the day, slow and reflective they all wandered back to their cars.

Piper found Gilbert at her side. 'He's a good bloke, eh?' he said quietly.

She grinned and couldn't disagree.

Chapter 13

Piper and Ben travelled in his four wheel drive back to the roadhouse to collect the artwork and her car.

'Can you believe all this is over?' she said.

'It's been a journey.'

In more ways than one, she reflected. 'There's no way I can-'

'I know.' He reached out across the gear shift and rested a hand on her leg, briefly sparing a glance from focusing on the road to give her one of his disarming smiles.

'One question though. How did the men find you?'

Ben chuckled. 'You wouldn't believe it but they put a tracker on the motorbike. The bike led them to the garage. I don't blame Pete. According to Hendry, he had a gun levelled at his head.'

Piper clutched her throat. 'That's why our escape was so easy at the airfield. Not so dumb after all.'

Before they left the four wheel drive, as they pulled into the roadhouse carpark beside her old

Holden, Ben eased his mind by phoning Pete at the garage in Dunkeld. After a brief conversation, ensuring the old man was okay, he hung up again.

'Good news then?'

Ben nodded but hesitated before climbing out. 'I hope we can stay in touch.'

Her heart rolled over with pleasure. 'I'd like that. We already have each other's mobile numbers.' Be interesting to see where that led. She couldn't wait.

Piper transferred her backpack into her car then they strolled together into the restaurant.

Holly beamed the moment she caught sight of them. 'You're back safe. Everything okay?'

'Absolutely. This is my friend Ben. He's a private investigator and helped me sort out our family problem.' She turned to him. 'Holly Duncan. And Gracie has been babysitting our treasure in their safe.'

'Holly,' Ben acknowledged with a nod.

'Pleased to meet you. Ben,' she emphasised with a cheeky side grin to Piper. When he glanced up at the menu board behind the counter, Holly raised her eyebrows toward Piper in approval, as if to say *Hello soldier* and gave a thumbs up.

Piper rolled her eyes. He did look sexy and rugged in camouflage cargos and that windcheater. A thick shadow of face whiskers.

She sighed then leaned toward him and

said, 'Just so you know, in case you're considering a food order, Mum will have a feast prepared. A meat-stacked barbeque with all the country trimmings.'

'Noted. Might grab a chicken burger for the road, Holly. A man needs to keep up his strength,' he drawled, grinning down at Piper.

The dare in his deep voice clearly told her *you can take that any way you please.*

Piper blushed. While his order was made up, she asked Holly, 'Gracie in her office?' She nodded. 'I'll be right back.'

After weaving her way along the rear passage again – so much had happened, it felt longer than only a few hours ago – Piper tapped on Gracie's half open office door and pushed it wider.

Gracie glanced up over her red glasses, her face crinkling into a broad smile. 'Piper. Knew you'd be back.' She was already rising and heading for the wall safe, stepping aside when it was unlocked.

Drawing out the cylinder with care, Piper felt the need to explain its significance to Gracie. The importance of what she had held in trust. If only briefly. Gracie Townsend and her brother, Sid, had owned and run this roadhouse for decades. Both well-known lifetime district citizens.

'There's a fragile piece of traditional indigenous bark artwork in this roll. We believe it could be anything up to a hundred years old and is clearly priceless. In more ways than one. It was stolen five years ago and has been missing ever since. At the time, I looked suspicious and blame was unjustly cast on me by association. You knew my grandma Thorne who died recently?'

'Of course, my dear. I had the pleasure to meet and talk to her many times over the years. She was an interesting woman. We'll all miss her deeply.'

'She left me a letter with a possible lead to the artwork's recovery. I've been following up that clue with the help of a private investigator who was supposed to find me and turn me in to the people connected to the artwork's theft in the first place. But we teamed up instead and, today, we found it and got it back.'

Gracie clasped her hands together. 'Piper, that's quite a story. What an amazing positive end to it all.'

'We're having a handing over ceremony to celebrate its return to my father again, the Elder entrusted with its care now.'

'Maybe something this precious should be kept in a safer place?' Gracie suggested carefully.

'My thoughts exactly. I intend to raise it with Jimmy tonight.' Piper raised the artwork. 'Thank you for being part of its return journey to us.'

'Always my pleasure, dear.' Gracie hugged her warmly. 'Don't be a stranger,' she hinted. 'Come and say hello whenever you're passing through.'

Piper returned to the restaurant to find Ben patiently waiting and munching on his burger.

'Just explaining to Gracie the meaning and my appreciation for what she was holding for us. Even if it was only for a few hours.'

Before leaving the restaurant, Piper wandered through to the mini market at the far end to buy a bunch of winter flowers. Red lillypilly leaves tucked brightly in among curly spikes of grevillea, stunning orange banksia and frothy white stalks of thryptomene, the native birth flower for June. The sandy Grampians soil was ideal for growing native plants.

In the carpark outside, Piper said to Ben, 'I want to make a stop on the way home. Something I need to do first before encountering crowds of family.'

'Should I tag along?'

'Probably. You don't know the area. You might get lost,' she teased. 'But when we get there, I'll need to be alone.'

He shrugged. 'Sure.'

On the highway driving toward Horsham, with Ben in sight not far behind, Piper felt protected. No longer haunted by criminals and thieves. She grinned to herself and turned the radio onto country music, the precious artwork tucked securely into her backpack on the passenger seat beside her.

On the edge of town, Piper pulled up outside the fence of the lawn cemetery. Carefully gathering up the artwork and the flowers, she climbed from her vehicle. Ben pulled up alongside and wound down his window. His tender expression told her he had guessed her intentions.

She longed to hug him for his concern. 'I won't be long.'

'I'll be here,' he murmured easily.

Good to know. For how long though, Piper wondered?

Carrying the precious cylinder, Piper passed through the gates and along the rows, walking toward her grandma's grave. Her heart pounded with apprehension and excitement. Being her first visit since the funeral day, the site was still brimming with flowers including native bunches and drying branches of slender eucalypt leaves.

Piper's composure crumbled at the mere sight of it all as she knelt to place her floral tribute beside the others. 'Grandma, I can't believe it only took three weeks but we found it. We did it. You and Ben and I.' She held out the cylinder, imagining her grandma could see.

Tears of sorrow and happiness rolled down Piper's cheeks as she spilled out all that had happened to her in recent weeks.

'Did you send me a guardian angel? Because

I didn't do it alone. Ben found me. I know you can hear me so I'm just here to thank you for all your efforts before you left us. None of us will ever know the effort of work it must have taken you into finding that breaking lead that got me started. While you were sick. That's courage and devotion, grandma.

'Thank you for your letter and believing in me when many others didn't. It was a shock to see your spidery handwriting. Like you were there speaking to me. You only learnt to read and write when you were older and you never did get the hang of neatness, did you?' Piper smiled through her flood of grief.

'I love you so much and always will. I am so proud you're *my* grandma. You're a sister role model I admire and respect. I'll try to live up to the standard you've set. It's how I want to live my life. For my family. Never be afraid to stand up for what's right and speak out.'

Piper sniffed and wiped her face. Closed her eyes and took deep breaths, feeling the nippy winter breeze brush over her skin. Allowing the moment to calm her soul and heavy heart. It would be July soon and she would return to the milder weather by the sea. Oddly, that thought caused her mixed feelings.

Piper pushed herself to stand. 'Bye, grandma.'

She blew her a kiss and tucked the cylinder into her fleece jacket, wandering back to her old

Holden in an emotional daze. Ben leant against his vehicle, legs and arms folded, waiting.

'She knows,' Ben whispered, sliding an arm around her shoulders when she came to stand beside him in silence.

He didn't press for anything more from her. He recognised his presence alone was enough. Just to have another human being there that she cared for and trusted.

Piper breathed deeply. In and out. Gradually, she became aware of her surroundings again and the passing of another grey winter day. No sun, as if to mirror her heavy feelings. They would ease but she wanted to be strong for the forthcoming family gathering. It did not promise to be small.

After a while, Piper said softly, 'Are you ready for an onslaught of Thornes?'

'Why not,' he chuckled.

'I'll lead the way.'

Ben followed Piper to her parent's farm cottage a few kilometres away on the eastern fringe of town.

'You've been a dark horse.' Kirra launched herself at her older sister as Piper and Ben walked toward the house, trusty backpacks slung over their shoulders. 'You didn't go back to the coast at all. Dad told us where you've been.' Her voice lowered to a whisper and tears pooled in her eyes. 'And why. We can't believe you got it back. Everyone's talking about it.'

'I hope they also know Coen was implicated,' Piper said crisply. 'Maybe now he's been exposed, he won't be quite so smug in future.'

Kirra stood back in admiration. 'You've toughened up.'

'Came with the territory.' Piper stepped aside, conscious that Ben was being completely neglected. 'My sister, Kirra. Woman of many words and even more opinions.'

At the sight of her sister's companion, Kirra's eyes glazed over and silently conveyed *Yum*.

Thinking it best to drag him away, Piper said to Ben, 'I'm sure you could do with a long hot shower.'

'You're not wrong.'

'I'll show you the main bathroom. Give you time to unwind before you're besieged with fans.'

'Do you want to tidy up first?'

'I can use my parents' ensuite.'

Piper strode through the house, waving to her mother and the ladies in the kitchen in passing. 'Back later.'

'I'm happy to camp out anywhere tonight,' Ben said in the hallway.

'You abandoned your tent when we left the valley in a hurry.'

'I've slept under the stars before.'

'On a winter's night?' He shrugged and

grinned. 'Of course you have.' She indicated the bathroom. 'I'll introduce you around when you're done.'

Fifteen minutes later, they both emerged, fresher and dressed in clean clothes. They almost collided in the hallway. Piper caught her breath in awe and their gazes held.

'Even Ella will be impressed,' she murmured, looking him up and down. 'Come and meet my mother.'

In the kitchen, huge trays of roast vegetables were browning to a delicious crisp in the ovens, and pots of broccoli and minted peas steamed on the stovetop. Bowls of salads were being tossed together and still-warm damper, just removed from among the coals in the central outdoor fire pit, were being pulled apart or thickly sliced.

Piper was more than aware of the work and preparation involved in producing all this for the festive evening barbeque. In honour of herself and Ben. If she was honest, personally she didn't feel worthy. Just did what had to be done when the opportunity opened. But also knew that, thanks to her grandma, she had earned the tribute.

This is the way her mother expressed her care and love. And probably thanks, although she would never voice it. Ella Thorne worked hard for her family and community, yet rarely showed emotion. Piper accepted this was her mother's nature, had always been so and would never change. At least not to any extent.

So she filled with a thread of hope when Ella settled her daughter with a heartfelt gaze, wiped her hands on her full apron and moved forward. There were no words. Piper was drawn into a brisk but genuine hug. She responded by wrapping her arms around her mother to enjoy the brief moment of simply being held. She couldn't remember the last time this had happened. Ella seemed to be saying *you did okay, kid*.

Maybe now, Piper thought, even though as the firstborn she was not the son her mother wanted, she might finally gain some respect. Her younger sister, Kirra, had been accepted and their young brother, Yarran, adored and spoiled. At least by his mother. Jimmy was more inclusive and spread his love around all three of his children.

She waited until her mother drew away again and immediately smiled at the man nearby. Piper's signal for an introduction.

'Mum, this is Ben Powell, the private-'

'I know who he is.' Piper flinched at the sharp comeback. 'My husband has told me what you have done for our daughter.'

'Sounds like she was misjudged five years ago,' Ben said carefully. 'Her cause was worthy and right to achieve justice. She needed the support.'

Piper glowed from the firm honesty in his

words. Confronted and speechless, her mother's eyes glazed over and she returned to the kitchen.

Always feeling unimportant in her mother's presence, Piper was grateful for the dismissal so they could escape. She led Ben outside into the crisp evening air. A thin sunset was underway between the clouds, Jimmy standing before the gigantic grandfather barbeque with chickens slowly roasting and basting on a long spit at one end. Sliced potatoes and onions were browning. The aroma hit the nostrils and made stomachs groan with hunger.

'Smells wonderful, Jimmy,' Ben said. 'Can I help?'

'No, young man, you're both our guests of honour tonight. Just enjoy yourself. Gilbert will be along shortly. He's a master cook, serve up your steak exactly how you like it. I'm just here to get things started. Can I get you a drink?'

'A beer would slide down well. Thanks.'

'Piper?'

'Same Dad.'

With beers in hand, Piper was unsure quite what to do with this handsome stranger in the midst of her wider family. She jammed one hand in the back pocket of her tight jeans. A long tunic sweater and thick wraparound scarf kept her body warm and her feet were cosily tucked into short black boots.

She had never been comfortable in large social gatherings and even less so to be the focus of the celebration. Should she start introducing Ben around? Fortunately, the awkward moment didn't last. Once word spread this was Piper's hero that helped save the mob's historic treasure, people stepped forward, hands were shaken in thanks and congratulations. Conversations buzzed and endless questions asked of them both.

Soon, Gilbert and Leyla with Gillie Junior sleeping and tucked up snug in a carry capsule, appeared around the corner of the house. They must have parked out front. Piper excused herself and strode across to meet them.

She hugged Leyla. 'Congratulations. You look wonderful.' Piper peeked among the folds of soft blankets. 'He's so tiny.'

'Eats and sleeps well. So far. We're blessed.'

Piper linked her arm through Gilbert's. 'Did the new father tell you what a hero he's been? Disarming the main thief with a strong arm and foot in the right places?'

Leyla smiled up at her husband. 'He wanted to help. You couldn't have kept him away.'

Gilbert sent her a warning glance. Seemed like he hadn't yet mentioned there was a gun involved. Piper flashed him a wink, conveying it would remain their secret. Her father wouldn't say anything and she hoped the boys had learnt enough from the gravity of their situation in the bush to keep their mouths shut. Apart from those involved, it didn't appear to be general knowledge yet about the underlying danger involved in Ben's rescue.

By now, most of their family had arrived. Piper noticed her brother, Yarran, tended to hover around their father and the older men which in itself was unusual. Coen was nowhere to be seen and she wondered why. Running late? Embarrassed?

With Gilbert's arrival, serious cooking was soon underway. He certainly had a way with a pair of barbeque tongs. Food from the kitchen ladies' efforts was carried out to fill a long side table. A line snaked along as everyone piled plates and retired to chairs surrounding the central fire pit, pushing out its radiant heat into the night.

Jimmy proposed a toast to Piper and Ben, everyone raised their glasses in accord and the welcome home barbeque was underway.

Ben stayed close to Piper, making her all too aware that eyes focused in their direction with interest. Her cousin Emma and sister Kirra angled their chairs nearby so the women could catch on their news of recent weeks.

Once the gathering ebbed to warming hot cuppas and legs stretched out toward the red coals in the fire pit, Piper knew it was time to broach a discussion with her father.

She approached Jimmy in a group of Elders, serious in murmured conversation. Waiting until a lull, she said, 'Dad, can I have a word?'

'Of course, dear.'

They stood to one side. As she wondered how to begin her suggestion, Jimmy said, 'Ben is an admirable young man.'

He would have noticed their kiss at the rescue in the bush. 'I agree.'

'You have a connection?'

'Early days.'

'This about him?'

'No, actually.'

'Spit it out,' he chuckled.

'When the artwork went missing, we thought it was lost forever. Did you know grandma was delving into it before she died?'

'No,' he admitted. 'She started working on a project but didn't share its purpose with anyone. We asked from time to time but she always casually passed it off. Her preoccupation went on for months, even when she grew frail toward the end. The family worried it was draining her health. During her last weeks, she seemed calmer. Wrote your letter which she entrusted to my care to pass along to you.'

'She was the artwork's current custodian,' Piper said. 'It must have weighed heavily on her mind. Not only that, because it's so significant to our culture, it will always remain nothing short of a miracle that we got it back. To be honest, Dad, I don't know if you've given it any thought, but the vulnerability of the artwork's future storage concerns me. Are you planning on keeping it in the house safe here again?'

'I understand your fear. We all know the artwork's value to us as a community but it's also a profitable prize for unscrupulous others. I hear where you're going with this.'

Piper relaxed. 'As custodian, I know it can be your decision alone and you may choose that path but do you think you could consult with other Elders and see what they think of our heritage artwork being placed for safe keeping on permanent loan into, say, an indigenous museum? With a full story of its history and *almost* loss. We need to highlight the scarcity and fragility of these types of rare and little known treasures and make them available for everyone to learn about. Besides, professional conservators could assess any potential restoration work so it survives in better condition for future generations to see and appreciate.'

Jimmy ran a thoughtful hand over his face. 'I take your point, Piper. It's a marvel to have the artwork back again. Maybe it's time for our family to surrender possession for its security but also its longevity in the history of our people. I'll arrange a meeting to discuss it. I'm sure they will give it genuine consideration with permission and approval to hand it on.'

Piper hugged her father in relief. 'Do you think we should lodge it in a bank vault until you decide? I mean, right now, it's back in our home office safe again and look how that turned out.' She tried to make light of the situation in order for her father to consider the urgency and gravity of the risky circumstances. 'Someone should guard that safe in person tonight and in the morning until after the handing over ceremony tomorrow afternoon. I'm happy to volunteer. Knowing what was involved in its rescue and the danger to my life and Ben's, I'd hate to think the artwork might disappear again.'

Jimmy frowned and considered his daughter with pride. 'Since I'm responsible now, I'll guard it myself. Set up a mattress in my office.'

'Dad, you're a sound sleeper,' Piper chuckled. 'Anyone could get past you.'

'Not if I set up a few hazards.'

Piper laughed and hugged him. 'I'm so glad you're my father.'

At that moment, perhaps seeing their private conversation was ending, Ben rose from his chair across the fire and approached them.

'Piper, when you're ready, maybe you could show me that camping spot.'

'Sure. Night Dad.'

They took separate vehicles across the paddock to the secluded site where Piper and her friends used to meet in a sheltered pocket of bush on the swamp. She dragged out a bundled hike tent retrieved from a farm shed and dumped it on the ground.

'You might want to pitch it sideways to the south wind coming in off the water. That way you still have a view out the front. You might even be treated to an eerie surface fog in the morning.' She wiggled her hands and grinned.

'You shouldn't have,' he teased.

Piper shrugged. 'There's room in the house but you insisted on being independent. Just trying to be neighbourly.'

'Your family have made me more than welcome.'

'You're their hero.'

'Am I yours, too?'

Challenged, Piper blushed. 'Of course.' After a pause, she said, 'Come up to the house for breakfast in the morning before we all head into town to give that statement to Ewan Holt.'

Ben steadily measured her from head to boots and gave a thumbs up. Self-conscious of his attention, she turned to head back to her car. Piper hadn't taken more than a few steps when she felt a hand on her arm.

'Piper-'

She halted and looked up into his dark eyes. Even beneath the shadowy gloom of the star-laden winter night sky, lit only by her vehicle headlights, intense invitation and promise clearly lingered on his face.

'Yes?' she whispered.

'Just want to say goodnight.'

Side on, he slid his other big strong arm around her waist and hauled her against him. Instinct made her stand on her toes, bringing their faces and especially their mouths, achingly close. She'd be a fool to resist, right?

The moment his cold lips touched hers, Piper's arms instinctively wrapped around him and her body heated from the contact despite thick clothing between them. It might be cold and calm outside in the open, but she was gripped by an explosion of deep burning emotions like no others she had ever known. For a man she had only met days before.

Ben's passionate kissing rocked her world. Her response didn't really come as a shock. It had been building since first sight of him in the bush carpark when he had bailed her up. Believing him the enemy. Who knew?

After long wonderful moments of teasing and exploration, and straying hands finding warm bare skin beneath clothing, they reluctantly drew apart.

'Probably no way to treat a lady,' he drawled.

'Clearly, I'm not always a lady.'

'I'm not always a gentleman myself.'

'Good to know. For future reference,' she added, surprising herself to feel so cheeky.

'I'll hold you to that.'

There would be more? This *thing* between them, whatever name you gave it, really was moving fast. She didn't want him to think less of her after all he had done. He knew how much he had done for her but still... 'Ben,' she paused, 'I don't want to ruin our friendship.'

He flashed her a wide sexy smile. 'I have other friends.'

Piper threw back her head and laughed. The sound carried softly across the night. 'Tomorrow's a busy day. Get a good night's sleep.'

'After a kiss like that?'

'You started it.'

She turned and strolled with swinging hips back to her car, knowing he was watching her every sassy step of the way.

No surprise, after tossing and turning, it took her quite some time to get to sleep.

Chapter 14

Next morning at breakfast, Piper found it an effort to avoid Ben's gaze across the room. She tried for casual, begging her eyes not to stray in his direction. At least, not too often. Remembering how Ben had kissed her long and slow, heating up and discovering each other.

Especially with Kirra's razor sharp glances and knowing grins turned her way. Not to mention last night's interrogation from her sister about Ben when she returned from the swamp. Self-conscious and holding her new feelings to herself, Piper eventually faked a yawn, rolled over and pretended to sleep.

She wasn't ashamed of how she allowed herself to unravel last night or how she might have happily shared that hike tent. In fact, she was exhilarated.

After all that had gone down in the past month, losing her beloved grandma and the machinations involved in her mission to recover the family artwork, the liberation she felt to open up to her feelings for Ben and explore them brought her nothing but deep pleasure and a contentment she hadn't ever known. Scary and exciting.

The atmosphere was even more intense when Piper slid into the four wheel drive beside Ben and headed into town to the police station to give Ewan Holt their statements.

Jimmy had gone on ahead earlier, claiming a need to move cattle as soon as he returned. Piper wondered with amusement if it was her father being tactful again.

A tight wire of awareness strung between Ben and Piper. He would be leaving today after the handing over ceremony. What then? At the moment, she lived on the coast. He lived in the city. She avoided cities. And wondered where that left them. Simply as friends who might occasionally be in touch?

Piper ached to think she might only sometimes connect with Ben. If invited, could she face Melbourne's frenetic pace? Or would he come visit her on the coast? That last option appealed. Bottom line, she would leave it to Ben to decide.

Surviving the steamy mood in the car and once inside police headquarters, Piper soon discovered from Ewan Holt why Coen had been absent from the barbeque last night. Apparently, Coen's father and Jimmy convinced the boy he should go to the police and confess what he did all those years ago. They argued that, as a younger juvenile at the time, his age would be taken into account and might play in his favour if he worked with them in their enquiries. Since the art thefts had continued, they used the argument that his contribution might help the ongoing investigations and build a stronger case against the criminals.

It amused Piper to think that rebel Coen, usually full of bluster, had actually agreed to cooperate again.

So Ewan had personally questioned Coen, taking a detailed statement of the past theft in which he was involved and to what extent. Turned out, because of his indigenous connections, making theft of the indigenous bark artwork easier, Coen was deliberately targeted and introduced by a dodgy mate to Hendry and his offsiders who included Leo Taylor.

Apparently Coen was pumped for information. Being much younger and even more gullible back then, and maybe wanting to feel important, he blabbed about the artefact handed down through the Thorne family, sharing its exact location which he had covertly uncovered by stalking Piper in their house.

Under orders from Hendry, Leo Taylor had stolen it in reward for a cut of the eventual sale price.

'However, as we now know,' Ewan said, 'on the night it was taken, Leo had a warrant out against him for another crime. He was pursued and captured by a police unit at his shack in the

Grampians but not before he had a chance to hide the original cylinder and its precious contents.

'The art theft team are working on those higher up in the chain of command in the organisation. As we speak, Hendry's haggling over terms of a reduced sentence if he gives up the name of the buyer in the plane who seems to be a big player and probably closely connected and next down to the top guy. If not his personal client and collector.

'All four men we arrested are up on charges. Vince and Eddie will likely be bailed. There's a strong possibility Taylor's going straight back to prison. Hendry's too important to be released and is still in custody.

'Coen Thorne was discharged with a warning. Now he knows the seriousness of his loose tongue, even if he was innocently coerced and manipulated, that may be enough to deter him from any future criminal tendencies. We certainly hope the young man changes his ways.'

Ewan glanced across the interview room table to Piper. 'Unless you have some ideas of a form of discipline since you, personally, and your family, were the people most affected by his actions. Although the entire community equally suffered the loss.'

'Sounds like he's been through enough.' Piper reflected a moment. 'When Gilbert and I questioned Coen, trying to re-establish a trail back to Leo, at least Coen finally told the truth. Reluctantly, it must be said,' she grinned, 'but at least he sent me in roughly the right direction to find Leo and Vince in the southern Grampians. And he helped – or more likely was persuaded - to take part in the mission to free Ben.

'Together with Yarran, he actually proved useful in overpowering Eddie. Maybe the boy's attempt at restitution is proof of his regret over what he did when he was so much younger and more easily influenced. Now the truth is out, I believe my father and the other community Elders should decide.

'Even though your family theft happened years ago,' Ewan said, 'it's still an offence to possess objects of cultural heritage knowing them to be stolen. So your case is still valid and applies to our ongoing and current investigations on the matter of the other associated crimes.'

Piper and Ben's detailed statements, as far as they remembered from everything that had gone down recently in connection with the artwork recovery, and Piper's memories of her every movement on that fateful night years before, were being typed up ready for signatures.

'Even though your particular case is an historical one,' Ewan said, 'you can be assured this information will go far to assisting us in eventually nailing the criminals in the illegal theft syndicate.'

As they left the police station, Piper felt satisfied that the law finally knew about their stolen community artwork. Perhaps their family should have reported it back when it first happened. Kudos to her father for taking the initiative and informing them when he did two days ago. Exposing the thieves still in action five years later and probably even earlier, leading to vital police backup and successfully freeing Ben.

'You're quiet,' Ben said as they drove back to the farm.

'Lots to think about,' Piper said. 'You heading home after the ceremony?'

'To be honest, not sure it feels like home anymore,' Ben admitted. 'Even after less than a week.'

She was surprised to hear it but sensed a similar indifference for herself about returning to the coast. The Wimmera was her ancestral country, a strong link to her people, and she would always think of it as *home* but, for now, she still felt the need to wander. Explore further afield. Although maybe rethink always doing it alone.

She had casual and loyal friends in her art world but had now experienced the depth of difference in the close company and friendship of a man who had literally captured her attention and, in the process, kick started her heart. Without any doubts, in such a short time, proving himself worthy of her responding attraction in every way.

More amazing still, with whom she would risk falling in love. Piper caught her breath at the thought. This pull of chemistry between them was real and mutual. It would be the biggest wrench to surrender that. She believed she already knew his feelings. He had made them perfectly clear. So, it all depended on the depth of Ben's desire to pursue their relationship. If anything even came from this heady new power neither could resist.

For now, Piper was forced to shelve her concerns about the future for Ben had turned off the main feeder road from town, through the open property gate and onto the gravel track that led to the farm cottage.

The extended family shared lunch leftovers from last night before the community began arriving again. A ceremony was often held when something important was returned to their people so they all pitched in setting up for handing over the newly rescued artwork down by the swamp.

When it was time for the proceedings to start, Ben went on ahead with most of the others while Jimmy unlocked the house safe, Piper by his side. She withdrew the cylinder and together they carried it slowly and with respect across the paddock to the prepared site of the imminent ritual.

The small crowd parted as they approached, Piper holding out the cylinder in front of her. As she and her father stepped into the middle of the gathering, she deliberately searched and found Ben, steadily holding his gaze. He knew how much this meant and his significant personal contribution. He gave a nod as he smiled and her heart tumbled with happiness.

One man lit a bundle of tied twigs and bent to ignite a pile of eucalyptus leaves in a ceremony pit, a hollowed-out area in the ground that immediately produced thick smoke. Those gathered formed a circle, then each person in turn moved forward, wafting the smoke around them with their hands to acknowledge the ancestors, ward off evil spirits and cleanse this special place.

When the solemn formality was done, it signalled the moment when Piper said a few words to officially hand over and return the lost artwork to her father on behalf of their kin.

'I am honoured to have this opportunity to return this sacred cultural heritage item back to the place where it belongs. I would like to acknowledge my grandma Thorne whose efforts led to this homecoming today and who was the previous custodian of our ancestral artwork. And to my good friend, Ben Powell. This ancestral treasure would not be in our hands today without his help.'

Piper's father received the cylinder with a nod and smile. 'I accept the return of this gift on behalf of my people. It has been decided that such a valuable icon should find a permanent place within an indigenous living cultural centre where it will be protected and shared for all people to enjoy.'

Piper wasn't surprised to hear it. Jimmy had been efficient in gathering support for his decision, easing pressure on the artwork's safe and lasting conservation.

Finally, the circle was complete again. The artwork where it should be. Her relationship with her mother, Ella, fragile yet showing a glimmer of potential growth. They may never be close but at least Piper sensed a measure of adjustment underway.

With the formal part of the occasion over, Piper accepted warm hand clasps of gratitude from her people. She noticed Ben equally besieged by the community members. Recognition, now the facts were known, that she had played no part in the artefact loss years ago and yet was instrumental in its repossession.

Always close by, Piper made sure Ben was drawn into conversations, pointing out his vital leading role on their mission.

Beer and cuppas were offered at the farm cottage so everyone trailed back. A happy occasion. Wandering at their leisure, chattering with excitement.

Although deep in reflection, Piper instinctively sensed when Ben fell into step beside her. She knew a crazy thrill of pleasure that he constantly sought her out. She liked being wanted.

With his hands sunk into his pockets, still unshaven yet looking ridiculously handsome as no man had a right to be, Piper asked, 'You staying for yet another Thorne feast?'

'Do you want me to?'

'Of course. You're honorary family now, remember?'

Neither looked at the other as they spoke, both suddenly finding fascination in the damp grass beneath their feet. A sharp wind had whipped up off the swamp as the ceremony progressed. Together with gathering clouds, the grey winter day promised to turn bleak. At least they had their backs to the biting southerly as they walked.

From here on, every moment in Ben's company, Piper considered a bonus since the future loomed full of unknowns.

The afternoon gathering stretched toward evening. Ben still hadn't made any move to leave. Some community members lingered but most had already left.

Piper hugged the hope Ben might stay longer. Since both of them were self-employed, work pressures weren't a particular concern. But her anticipation was dashed when he cast her a telling glance and drew her aside.

'You're leaving.'

'Had to happen. Delayed it as long as I could. I have a case situation in the pipeline. Need to get it underway.'

'Fair enough.'

'I've said my goodbyes and thanks to your folks.'

'Mum too?'

'Yep.'

'Charmer.'

He indicated toward his vehicle. 'Ride with me to the gate?'

Piper grinned. 'Sure.' She jumped into his four wheel drive again but he turned in the opposite direction. 'I hope you're kidnapping me.'

'My ultimate dream.'

'Really?'

'Letting you go for now but be warned,' he drawled.

The swamp, Piper noted as they approached. Of course. A peaceful private place.

'This vehicle knows its own way down here without GPS.'

She laughed. He pulled up facing the water's edge, climbed out and she followed. He sought her hand, linked fingers and stopped beneath an ancient gum. Ben leant against the trunk and dragged her into his arms. No time for words. He just started kissing her senseless.

Running his hands up into her short hair, trailing them lower over her backside. Pressing her against him. Piper groaned.

After being lost in their own world for quite some time, they eventually drew apart.

'Ben, you just driving away doesn't seem right. After all you've done.'

'I hear what you're saying and I'm okay with it. I'll never regret taking on Hendry as a client because I met you.'

'You bailed me up,' she teased. 'You actually intended handing me over to that bastard.'

'You fascinated me. You were so passionate about what you needed to do. I watched your mouth while you spoke with that glint of fire in those green eyes, and I was lost.'

'I had you at *hello*?'

'Something like that. Dripping with rain. You were gorgeous.'

'Keep talking.'

He fished out his phone. 'I have your mobile but not your address. Text it to me.'

Piper retrieved hers from a pocket and sent it. 'Yours?'

'You won't need it because I plan on haunting you at your place but, okay.'

Piper loved the promising sound of that. His text arrived. 'Albert Park. Nice suburb.'

'My folks bought it for a good price and renovated. I lived on my own digs once I returned from my wanderings but after my parents died I moved back into the family home. You know the story.'

Piper nodded and let him continue.

'When you asked me earlier today if I was heading home, it hit me how much one week can change a life. I followed and found you in the bush and we went on this crazy ride together. I wouldn't swap a second of time I've been with you.'

'Me either,' Piper whispered, her body humming at his warm words.

'Soon as you're down on the coast again, I'll come visit.'

'So, the sooner you leave, the sooner I can leave, and the sooner I get to see you again. Sound right?' She flashed him a cheeky grin.

'You catch on fast,' he murmured and started up with the kissing goodbye thing again, leaving Piper breathless and nothing to the imagination.

'At this rate, we're never going anywhere,' she chuckled.

'Okay. I'll leave so you can leave. To be continued.'

Piper couldn't wait. Even as Ben dropped her at the cottage again and drove away, she already missed him. The future looked promising but she grew anxious over the difficulty of living so far apart. How many distance relationships ever really worked and survived?

Somehow, she figured because they both wanted it, they would manage it between them. But right now, she hadn't a clue how it would happen.

Chapter 15

Jimmy and Ella Thorne were nothing short of staggered when they found their oldest daughter packing that night.

'Need to get back to my life and work on the coast,' she said.

Kirra begged to come visit one weekend soon. Could turn awkward, Piper thought, if Ben was there too. Splitting herself between her sister and her boyfriend.

So Piper merely left her with a promise that she would arrange it once she was resettled. As yet, she was ignorant how that outlook would develop. How much Ben could become a part of her future.

On the drive south to the coast later, Piper felt foolish to have even doubted Ben's commitment when texts kept pinging her phone. There were so many, she kept pulling over to stop, read and respond to them.

'You realise this is harassment,' she wrote back.

'*I can stop.*'

'No!'

'Tell me when you arrive so I know you're safe.'

'That a dig about my old car?'

'Only concerned about you.'

'Are you working?

'I am. Working on seeing you again.'

Strange answer. And so it went on for the entire three hour journey. By the time Piper finally pulled into the driveway of her shared coastal flat, across the road from a stunning endless beach, she was elated and exhausted.

Ben hadn't forgotten her and it seemed unlikely that happy situation would change any time soon.

Piper unloaded the car. Her old Holden hadn't let her down the whole time she had been away but she made a mental note to book it in for a service anyway.

'You're home,' her flatmate Angie Wells exclaimed when she walked in the door.

Angie was your classic blue-eyed blonde but one of the strongest, most supportive and independent women Piper had ever been fortunate enough to meet. A fellow artist she had encountered at a weekend retreat, Angie was one of the few constants in her life.

'Hey Ange.' They hugged warmly.

Holding her at arm's length, Angie said, 'Looks like the break did you good. I thought you'd be miserable since the funeral. I know how close you were to your grandma.'

Piper sighed and said carefully. 'Kind of sad

and happy, I guess.'

'Really? Want a cuppa?' Piper shook her head. 'Beer?' Piper nodded.

Before they had barely sprawled on the sofa for a catch up chat, Piper's phone began beeping with messages again. She tried to tactfully ignore it. Devoting her attention to Angie instead but the pinging continued.

'Sorry.' Piper wrinkled her nose, feeling hot, sure her face was flushed. 'Better take this.'

She escaped into the privacy of her room to reply, assuring her persistent admirer – was he officially her boyfriend? – she was safely home. Flustered to be feeling so preoccupied and smitten by this man.

She immediately agreed to Ben's first visit to her coastal home, pressing down on her loved up excitement to be seeing him again so soon. Early the following Friday according to his latest text.

Returning to the living room again where Angie had half finished her beer, Piper felt the need to explain. 'A friend just checking I'm okay.'

A slow grin spread across Angie's face. 'You've met someone!'

'You're so nosy.'

Angie laughed. 'How else can I learn anything? You keep stuff close.'

Her flatmate's big blue eyes appealed for more.

'It's a long story,' Piper warned.

'Do I look like I'm busy?'

So Piper settled back and told it. All the highs and lows, embellished with confessed snippets of her budding attraction. Holding Angie's undivided attention, interrupted by her friend's regular gasps and exclamations of surprise at the dicey moments, and watery eyes at the revelation of finding her family's treasure.

'You sure filled in your time while you were away and fancy meeting such a spunk in the bush. In the middle of nowhere. So he's city, you're country. How will that work?'

Exactly Piper's dilemma. Unable to answer, she shrugged.

'Will I ever meet him?'

Piper flashed a crafty grin. 'Next Friday apparently.' Angie's mouth opened but Piper went on quickly. 'So give us some space, okay?'

'Cruisy. Done.' Angie shook her head. 'Piper Thorne, you're a dark one. Hot for a guy after a week.'

Piper moaned, resigned to being watched and teased all week. Shutting herself in her studio, a renovated garden shed at the rear of their flat and trying to focus on painting again seemed her best bet to avoid Angie and her own crazy anticipation. A tough ask on both fronts but she'd give it a shot.

Would the weekend live up to her hyped-up imagination, Piper wondered? She woke with the Friday sunrise spreading its golden glow across the water like a glassy path from horizon to beach. She had finished three new paintings for the week. So, technically, she was free for the weekend. A month ago, her Saturdays and Sundays tended to blur into weekdays. A heady change to be actually taking time off.

Piper showered and dressed then forced herself to be patient. Not easy when she was so full of nervous energy. Winter had turned on a classic sunny day but the south wind blowing onshore felt like the Antarctic and held bite.

Over coffee with Angie before her friend disappeared, Piper reflected on the sexy sound of Ben's voice on the other end of his phone calls during the week. Double checking details, he claimed. Confirming her address. That she would be home when he arrived. And simply to talk. It all seemed so fresh and uncomplicated, Piper worried it might all come crashing down.

Then an unfamiliar vehicle pulled up on the street. Piper's heart set up a frantic thud before she relaxed and grinned at the sight of his wheels.

She pulled on a coat over jeans and boots, wound a scarf around her neck and stepped onto the front porch. With the deepest sense of indulgent pleasure, she gawked at Ben as he unfurled himself from a soft top two-door Jeep. Yellow.

She wagged her finger and shook her head,

laughing. 'You teased me about my old Holden. Which I consider unique.' She nodded toward his vehicle. 'Your wheels are equally rad. And those big tyres.' She whistled low. 'I may need a step ladder to get up into that thing.'

Piper decided not to tell him the off-roader was actually full of character and oddly cute.

Ben grinned, posing in front of it. 'My weekender. Like it?'

'You're wicked.'

Understandable how he had so easily slid under her skin. When he was around she didn't even bother to hide her emotions. That would take too much energy which she planned on saving for more worthy pursuits. His arms hung loose as he strolled toward her. The entire rugged package held her still.

'Hey,' he drawled.

He smelt fresh and earthy as he hauled her into his arms. His red-blooded kiss was lusty and loaded with promise. Just how she had grown to like it. Were they on the same page or what?

'So, I'm guessing you're Ben?' a cheeky voice chirped from behind.

Piper groaned as they drew apart. 'Angie, meet Ben. Ben, my flatmate Angie Wells.'

'Pleasure to meet you.'

'My pleasure, too,' Angie rolled her eyes. 'Just leaving and for goodness sake, Piper,' she threw over her shoulder, 'have fun.'

Arms around each other as Piper's friend strode away, Ben called out, 'I'll make sure of it.'

Piper landed him a gentle punch then stood on tiptoe and kissed him again. 'I'll give you the guided tour and show you my studio out back. Won't take long.'

'No rush. We have all weekend.'

Piper hadn't realised how small the flat actually was until Ben wandered through with her. Every time they brushed against each other, it was like a spark that ignited heat and consumed her. It felt as though Ben was just being polite, going through the motions, biding his time. Taking it slow. Giving Piper emotional space now they were together again. And she appreciated it. Realising she needed to settle her composure. Her attraction was so deep and overwhelming for this guy, she used the moments to simply ease back into the enjoyment of his company once more.

First sight of him had been like a fresh breeze on her skin and had taken her breath away. Was this love? So soon? Whatever, it felt amazing.

In her studio Piper humbly stood aside, letting Ben take in her work. Her latest painting rested on her easel, a reflective bush watercolour bathed in slanting light at its centre with subtle indigenous symbols woven through.

'Wonderful,' he murmured.

'Thanks. My work is on paper and canvas

but traditional indigenous art could be rock art and ochre paintings, often on cave walls and overhangs, wood carvings and sculptures. Or on bark like the family piece we recovered. All the more special because bark is so fragile and lacks longevity.

'You know, indigenous art is the oldest form of artistic expression in the world. It's filled with symbols and icons. We don't have a formal written language so artwork is central to our culture because it's a visual story. Brown and orange tones represent the earth, and blue tones represent the ocean.'

Ben glanced around the studio. 'I've noticed you use a lot of that colour in your coastal paintings.'

'Like green, I find it's a peaceful colour.'

'How did you get started in painting?'

'Grandma Thorne's encouragement since childhood. I was always fascinated by Albert Namatjira's work. The soft pastel colours. His ghost gums with their white trunks and the purple-blue hills in the background. Just loved them.'

The charged atmosphere between them highlighted a brief lapse in conversation. Not uncomfortable, still Piper grew restless to get out and really live every precious moment of her limited time with this amazing man.

She didn't much care where they went but before she could voice her thoughts, Ben said,

'Shall we take a spin along the Great Ocean Road?'

Piper smiled. 'I think we should.'

She grabbed her puffer coat and they were on the road in minutes. Seated beside Ben in supreme contentment as they snaked along the winding beachside lane around the base of cliffs, Piper took in the dramatic beauty of the windswept southern ocean.

She contemplated the thousands of returned soldiers after World War 1 who helped build it over thirteen years, living in bush camps along the way, as a memorial to their fallen comrades.

From time to time, Ben pulled into a viewing area. Piper hugged her coat closer as the stiff wind streamed by them while they drank in breathtaking views. Hugging each other close with affection and for warmth.

When they grew hungry, they stopped for lunch of fresh crumbed fish and chips, eaten in a sheltered corner of a beach. Ben licked Piper's fingers, his eyes dark and mischievous with intent.

By late afternoon, they were heading back along the oceanfront in the opposite direction.

'Best times of day are dawn and dusk,' Piper murmured, deeply satisfied in Ben's company.

Before they reached her town, he stopped in a layover for a lonely endless beach.

Piper sat up. 'What's here?'

'Us.'

Ben slid out, so she followed, to watch him rummage in the rear, shrug on a backpack, a bag of driftwood in one hand and holding out the other to her in invitation.

Piper took his strong warm grasp and they sauntered down onto the sand. The pale day's sun no longer resisted the pull of the horizon. Ben dropped his bundles. Hand in hand, they strolled the shore. The wind had dropped with the evening, the sky streaked with watercolour tints of apricot, yellow and mauve.

'So beautiful,' Ben said.

Piper's gaze turned out to sea. When she looked back at him to murmur her agreement, she realised he had been staring at her the whole time and blushed.

'You just want my body,' she whispered.

'True.' She was pulled tight and hungrily kissed. 'Let's go build a fire.'

Piper grinned. Double meaning there.

Ben soon had flames leaping then, of all things, produced and pitched his hike tent.

'You've come prepared.'

'I was a scout.'

They removed their coats and footwear, snuggled together in the tent opening, their bare feet stretched out onto the sand. With Ben's arm around her shoulder and his warm breath against her hair, Piper knew there was nowhere else in the world she would rather be.

The situation reminded her of their bush

camp at the mountain valley airfield when she wondered at the cosy fit of two people in a one man tent. On that occasion, it hadn't happened. Tonight, she would find out.

Mesmerised by each other against a backdrop of stunning sunset colours, Piper let Ben's kisses carry her to that heady place all lovers know. The fire died to coals but not their passion. Half in and half out of a sleeping bag, Ben stoked her desire to heights that left her gasping.

They dozed, waking to the excitement of a warm body nestled against the other and, in a hot rush, made love again.

Sometime later, even their physical activity wasn't enough to keep the winter cold at bay. They packed up the tent, Ben smothered the fire with sand and they walked briskly back to the Jeep.

Over a late night roadhouse snack and coffee, Piper said, 'My place?'

Ben nodded. When they arrived, the flat was in darkness.

Piper frowned. 'Unusual for Angie to be asleep this early.'

Inside, she found a note propped up on the kitchen counter and chuckled. 'Angie is staying with friends for the weekend.'

So followed two days of loved up bliss. Piper was well aware they had only known each other a few weeks. Yet she couldn't deny their burning attraction was deeply felt and real. Ben had certainly confirmed that impression in every way.

So they spent much of their time grinning at each other, holding hands and stealing kisses in the happy glow of new love. More rewarding was the simple pleasure of being in Ben's company. Talking. Sharing.

Even knowing Ben was working on a new assignment, Piper still considered Sunday evening arrived far too soon.

'Might be a week or two before I get back,' he warned at the Jeep while they stretched out their goodbye.

Piper nodded. 'Stay safe.'

It was the toughest pull between happy and sad on her heartstrings watching his little yellow Jeep disappear from view.

Chapter 16

Piper's remedy to counter Ben's absence was to drive herself into her work, deliberately going to bed late, exhausted, so she could sleep.

After ten days, Angie frowned and teased at the same time. 'He's crazy about you. He'll be back.'

'I know. I hope he's missing me half as much as I'm missing him.'

'You know where he lives. You could surprise *him* with a visit,' Angie suggested.

Piper scrunched up her nose. 'You don't think it would be too pushy?'

Angie shrugged. 'Up to you.'

Piper hesitated. 'He's been texting and calling. He did say it might be a while before he could get back. I'll wait a few more days.'

By the second weekend following Ben's first sojourn on the coast and still no hint of a repeat visit, Angie dragged Piper from her studio and they sat out on the front porch, rugged up and drinking beers, the cloudy winter daylight slowly fading.

'I'm thinking pizza,' Angie said.

Piper blessed her flatmate for being so upbeat. 'I'm thinking that idea actually makes me feel hungry.'

'Good. You haven't been eating much lately.'

While Angie ordered their takeaway on her phone, Piper noticed the quiet of evening was mildly disrupted when a vehicle engine sound drew her attention. A white motorhome pulled up across two parking spaces on the beachside street.

Angie glanced up from her mobile. 'That's some comfortable home on wheels.'

When the driver's side door opened and a familiar man stepped down, Piper exclaimed with a small shriek of surprise. 'It's Ben.'

She was out of her chair in a flash and streaking across the road to meet him. He wrapped her in his arms, kissing her madly, and spun her around.

When he set her down, Piper gently prodded him with a finger. 'You didn't say you were coming.'

'Don't like surprises?'

'This one I can handle.'

'Sorry. I've been busy. Won't happen again.'

Piper's first negative thought was *he's travelling somewhere else on a job.* 'So, where you heading?'

'Here.'

'For the weekend?'

'Actually, my calendar is entirely free and open.'

Piper frowned.

'Come and have a look.' He indicated the camper.

Piper stepped inside and was immediately impressed. Everything appeared gleaming and new. Fully equipped. Truly a home on wheels.

She backed up against the compact kitchenette counter. 'Business must be doing well.'

'I've sold the family home in Albert Park and bought this instead.'

Piper's heart dropped. 'You'll be living on the road?'

'That's the plan.'

'How is that going to work with your job?'

'I'm more of a freelancer now.'

A sneaky suspicion slowly crept into Piper's mind. She held her breath and kept silent.

Because of the vibes humming between them, she suspected they had wickedly similar thoughts in mind. 'Bed looks comfortable.'

'Guarantee it.' Ben's suggestive gaze held hers. 'Stay with me tonight?'

'Does the invitation include breakfast?'

'It comes with all sorts of things.'

Piper's heart raced. 'Then I may just be tempted.'

'The answer I was hoping for. You ready for this?'

Piper smiled in memory. 'I seem to recall you challenging me like that another time.'

'I'm full of challenges.'

'So I've discovered.' Piper poked her head out the door and yelled across the street to Angie. 'Pizza is all yours. I've been kidnapped. I'm staying the night.'

'Shameless woman. The whole neighbourhood will hear,' Ben teased as he dragged her back inside, letting his hands skilfully deal with her clothes.

Much later, somewhere around midnight, as Ben nibbled her all over, he murmured, 'You know I've already tumbled head over heels for you, right?' Distracted, Piper mumbled something. 'I bought these wheels because I figured if we intend to keep hanging out together, I should upsize from the Jeep.' He raised himself on an elbow and studied her shadowed face in the half light. 'Wanna travel with me? Indefinitely? Destination unknown?'

Suddenly alert, Piper gasped at the challenging invitation and all of its heady possibilities. 'Us? In this?'

'Unless you have something against freedom. Skinny dips at night in a warm ocean-'

'Stop it!'

'Don't like the idea?'

'Bite your tongue. You could be a travel agent. I'm sold.'

'How soon can you pack in the morning?'

'I've always travelled light.'

The sun had barely peeped over the horizon, its golden rippled reflection skimming a path across the calm sea to shore, when Piper flew out of bed in the camper, dressed and sprinted across to the flat.

For the next hour, with Ben's help when he eventually surfaced, she grabbed most of her art supplies from the studio, a few armfuls of clothing and other belongings. Until only the most necessary of her humble possessions were safely stowed in her new home.

Breathless, bittersweet tears pooling behind her eyes, Piper said to Angie in the flat, 'This is all yours now.'

'All of it? The furniture we bought together?'

Piper slowly nodded, beaming. 'Everything I need is in that motorhome.'

'Way to go. Damn, I'll miss you like crazy.' They hugged.

No second thoughts. Only excitement filled Piper as she climbed up into the camper front seat beside Ben where they exchanged a tender glance.

Not driving off into the sunset but a sparkling winter morning and their future. And she couldn't wait to discover what lay ahead.

Whatever it was and wherever they went, it would be with Ben. And really, when it came right down to it, he was exactly what she wanted, and more than she could ever have hoped and dreamed.

www.ingramcontent.com/pod-product-compliance
Lightning Source LLC
Chambersburg PA
CBHW061032120726
47910CB00006B/2220

* 9 7 8 0 9 9 2 5 1 7 9 3 9 *